"Did you tell your sister about me?"

"About you?" he repeated, a little confused. Did she think that Megan would object to his planning things with her?

"Yes. About me," she said again. The silence on the other end told her that maybe she needed to elaborate on that before he got the wrong idea. "Did you tell her that I'll be playing at your parents' anniversary party?" The longer the silence on the other end of the phone, the tighter the knot that had suddenly come into being in her stomach became. A knot that had materialized for no apparent reason...

Isn't there a reason? something whispered in her head. *Haven't you caught him looking at you in a way that made you forget all about the music you were supposed to play and made you think about the music the two of you could produce, given half a chance?*

Dear Reader,

Well, the ladies are at it again. Those Matchmaking Mamas just can't help themselves. Confronted with a sad single, they become determined to turn that single into a duo. It just takes the right person, or in this case, the right man. It's what they love to do and feel they do best.

So when Maizie's old friend confides in her that he is concerned about his daughter who, in a moment of weakness, confessed that she felt as if she were relegated to the sidelines of life, Maizie is immediately off and running. A few discreet inquiries later and the ladies believe they have just the man for a perfect match. Now all it takes is moving a bit of heaven, a bit of earth and getting these two people together so that they could wind up making beautiful music together for life.

Wouldn't it be nice if it were that easy? Still, the heart is ever optimistic—and so am I. Once again, I would like to thank you for taking the time to read this, and from the bottom of my heart I wish you someone to love who loves you back.

All the best,

Marie Ferrarella

A PERFECTLY IMPERFECT MATCH

MARIE FERRARELLA

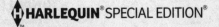
HARLEQUIN® SPECIAL EDITION®

Recycling programs
for this product may
not exist in your area.

ISBN-13: 978-0-373-65722-3

A PERFECTLY IMPERFECT MATCH

Printed in U.S.A.

Selected books by Marie Ferrarella

Harlequin Special Edition

¶*A Match for the Doctor* #2117
¶*What the Single Dad Wants...* #2122
***The Baby Wore a Badge* #2131
¶¶*Fortune's Valentine Bride* #2167
¶*Once Upon a Matchmaker* #2192
§§*Real Vintage Maverick* #2210
¶*A Perfectly Imperfect Match* #2240

Silhouette Special Edition

~*Diamond in the Rough* #1910
~*The Bride with No Name* #1917
~*Mistletoe and Miracles* #1941
††*Plain Jane and the Playboy* #1946
~*Travis's Appeal* #1958
Loving the Right Brother #1977
The 39-Year-Old Virgin #1983
~*A Lawman for Christmas* #2006
□□*Prescription for Romance* #2017
¶*Doctoring the Single Dad* #2031
¶*Fixed Up with Mr. Right?* #2041
¶*Finding Happily-Ever-After* #2060
¶*Unwrapping the Playboy* #2084
°*Fortune's Just Desserts* #2107

Harlequin Romantic Suspense

Private Justice #1664
†*The Doctor's Guardian* #1675
**A Cavanaugh Christmas* #1683
Special Agent's Perfect Cover #1688
**Cavanaugh's Bodyguard* #1699
*Cavanaugh Rules #1715
Cavanaugh's Surrender #1725
Colton Showdown #1737
A Widow's Guilty Secret #1736

Silhouette Romantic Suspense

†*A Doctor's Secret* #1503
†*Secret Agent Affair* #1511
**Protecting His Witness* #1515
Colton's Secret Service #1528
The Heiress's 2-Week Affair #1556
*Cavanaugh Pride #1571

**Becoming a Cavanaugh* #1575
The Agent's Secret Baby #1580
**The Cavanaugh Code* #1587
**In Bed with the Badge* #1596
**Cavanaugh Judgment* #1612
Colton by Marriage #1616
**Cavanaugh Reunion* #1623
†*In His Protective Custody* #1644

Harlequin American Romance

Pocketful of Rainbows #145
°°*The Sheriff's Christmas Surprise* #1329
°°*Ramona and the Renegade* #1338
°°*The Doctor's Forever Family* #1346
Montana Sheriff #1369
Holiday in a Stetson #1378
"The Sheriff Who Found Christmas"
°°*Lassoing the Deputy* #1402
°°*A Baby on the Ranch* #1410
°°*Forever Christmas* #1426

**Cavanaugh Justice
†The Doctors Pulaski
~Kate's Boys
††The Fortunes of Texas: Return to Red Rock
□□The Baby Chase
¶Matchmaking Mamas
°The Fortunes of Texas: Lost...and Found
°°Forever, Texas
**Montana Mavericks: The Texans Are Coming!
¶¶The Fortunes of Texas: Whirlwind Romance
§§Montana Mavericks: Back in the Saddle

Other titles by this author available in ebook format.

MARIE FERRARELLA

This *USA TODAY* bestselling and RITA ® Award-winning author has written more than two hundred books for Harlequin Books and Silhouette Books, some under the name Marie Nicole. Her romances are beloved by fans worldwide. Visit her website, www.marieferrarella.com.

To
Dr. Stephen Johnson,
for being
an excellent doctor all these years
and for giving me
a good idea

Prologue

"Well, I'm happy to report that all your lab tests came back totally normal," Dr. John Stephens said with a smile, closing Maizie Sommers's folder. He turned the stool he was sitting on so he was facing her directly. "If all my patients were as healthy as you and those two best friends of yours, I'd be forced to retire."

"Don't you dare," Maizie warned the man that she had known for the better part of thirty-five years, first as her family doctor, and then as a friend. "Doctors like you are hard to find in this day and age."

"You mean old?" He chuckled.

"No, I mean caring. And you're not old, John," she insisted, admiring his thick mane of silver hair and that endearing twinkle in his eyes. "As a matter of fact, there are times that you are quite possibly the youngest man I know."

The doctor could only shake his head and laugh.

Maizie had a gift for always saying the right thing at the right time. And he appreciated it, recognizing it for what it was: kindness.

"Then you definitely should get out more, Maizie," he urged. "That's my prescription for you—you need to broaden your base."

"My base is just fine, thank you," she assured him with a confident smile. "And you'll be happy to know that it most definitely *is* broad."

Seeing that she had managed to keep her trim figure over all these years, he could only interpret her comment one way. "Then your business is going well?" he asked. Glancing at his watch, he saw that he was running ahead of schedule and could allow himself a couple of moments to catch up.

After her husband had died, needing to provide for herself and her young daughter, he knew that Maizie had gone into the real estate business. She had done quite well for herself over the years and now owned her own company.

"Mercifully, yes. People still want to own their own homes, and I'm right there, eager to help them make their dreams come true." She never liked to focus on herself for more than a minute or so. She was far more interested in the people she was dealing with. Her doctor was included in this wide circle. "How are your children?" she asked in the same pleasant, unassuming tone. And as she asked, she studied his face, waiting for a response.

He moved her file from one side of his desk to another for no reason except that he seemed to need to do something with his hands. "They're healthy."

Maizie leaned in a little. "That's not quite what I asked, John."

He laughed, shaking his head. The woman was incredible. But then, he'd thought that on more than one occasion. "Sometimes I think you wasted your talent, going into real estate. You would have made one hell of a prosecutor."

"I don't like going after people. I like making them happy. And I *love* matching up houses and people, bringing them together. There is also my other interest," she reminded him with a subtle smile.

"Ah, yes, matchmaking." He recalled her telling him about that the last time she'd been in for her yearly checkup. "Are you still into that?"

"Yes," she said simply, wondering if he was going to ask her something a little less general, something that would address the nature of what had become her full-time hobby of sorts. "And so are Theresa and Cecilia," she told him, mentioning the women who had been her best friends since the third grade.

All three of them were businesswomen, all three of them were widows and all three of them reveled in matchmaking strictly for its own sake. Bringing two people together who seemed destined for each other was all the payment they really required.

"How's that going, anyway?"

The question sounded just a tad too innocently phrased. She studied him with interest. Had he finally admitted to himself that he was lonely? That he needed someone in his life? She was ready to help if he had.

"Our matchmaking business is doing very well. We still have that one hundred percent success record." She decided to stop beating around the bush and just come out with it. "Would you be interested in our services, John?" she asked quietly.

"Not personally," he protested, surprised at the question. For his part, he thought he was being very subtle about feeling her out on the subject. "At least, not for myself."

"I understand that, John," she assured him, silently adding, *And if you ever decide to change your mind, I'll be right here to help you.* Out loud she added, "I know you. You're a great deal like me. One life, one love. When your Annie died, you focused exclusively on your three children and your career."

He was surprised, with all the people she dealt with, that she would remember that. "You really are a remarkable woman, Maizie Sommers."

"So I've been told," she replied with a wide smile. And then she got down to business. "Now, which of your children is keeping you up at night?"

He didn't want to give Maizie the wrong impression. Nor did he want to be disloyal to Elizabeth. To the outside world, his daughter was outgoing, bubbly and very talented. She wasn't desperately trolling all the singles haunts, looking for a mate. His concern about her was due to something far more subtle.

"It's not that I'm worried about her. It's just that…" The doctor let his voice trail off, not knowing how to phrase what he wanted to say.

"You're worried about her," Maizie corrected, reading between the lines. "I thought Elizabeth was seeing someone."

He frowned, recalling his daughter's one serious relationship. "That's been over for a while. He was more interested in changing her than cherishing the person she was."

Maizie smiled, amused. "Spoken like a true doting father."

He supposed he was that. He loved all his children, but Elizabeth was his oldest and the only girl. She was the proverbial apple of his eye and he wanted to see her happy.

And she didn't seem to be.

"We had dinner the other evening and she confided that she felt as if life were bypassing her, because she was always supplying the background music for *other* people's romances."

Maizie summarized what was on his mind. "So, in essence, you'd like to find Mr. Perfect for her."

He surprised her by shaking his head. "No, I fully realize that there's never going to be a 'Mr. Perfect,'" he began.

Maizie cut him short. "Is that you being a realist, or you being a dad who feels that no man will ever be good enough for his daughter?"

He paused to consider that. "A little bit of both, I suppose, but mostly the second part," he confessed.

Maizie laughed. "All right, I'll see what I can do about finding Mr. Almost-Perfect for your daughter."

The doctor rose from his stool and walked Maizie out of his office. "I never thought I'd be one of those fathers looking to set their daughter up with someone. I mean, Elizabeth's talented, and beautiful—a passel of not-so-perfect men should be tripping all over themselves to get to her."

"Maybe they are." Maizie saw the look of surprise on the physician's handsome, patrician face. "Maybe Elizabeth's standards are exceptionally high. Maybe," she concluded, "she's trying to find someone as upstanding, kind and decent as her father."

That had never occurred to him. "You really think that's why she's still single?"

"Most likely not consciously, but, John, you are a hard act to preempt," Maizie told him, then added with a wink, "But don't worry, I am going to try my darndest to do just that."

"I don't know whether to be relieved, or worried," he said honestly.

"Just continue being who you are, John," she soothed gently, then promised, "I'll get back to you soon."

With that, she left his office, a cheerful woman with a mission.

Chapter One

Her fingers glided flawlessly over the taut strings of her violin.

Little by little, as she played, Elizabeth Stephens felt the same old longing creeping over her, the desire to be *part* of the party instead of merely providing the music *for* that party.

The moment she realized that her mind had drifted, and that she was feeling way too sorry for herself, Elizabeth winced with guilt.

Here she was, not just stitching together a passable living allowing her to make ends meet, but happily making a very decent living.

Oh, she couldn't go put a down payment on a yacht anytime soon, but she was more than just getting by—while others in her chosen field had either been forced to give up their dreams entirely, or were doing it more as a hobby that they tried to fit in around their day job.

Luckily, *her* day job also featured playing the violin. She managed to make a good salary by melding a couple or so different varieties of orchestra engagements. One gig involved playing in the pit for a theater group that was currently trying their hand at a revival of *Fiddler on the Roof,* another entailed being part of a six-piece orchestra that periodically was called in to provide the background music being scored for a romantic-comedy series.

The last gig involved working alongside several musicians on a commercial for an insurance company. It paid double because they not only played the music but were also *seen* playing. Her brother Eric had teased her about her screen "presence" and had asked her for her autograph.

And all those jobs didn't include the weddings, anniversaries, graduation ceremonies and various other social engagements that regularly came her way.

Like this one, Elizabeth thought, taking care to keep her smile in place as she and the four other entertainers who had been hired to perform at Barry Edelstein's Bar Mitzvah began playing yet another song.

It wasn't the thirteen-year-old who had triggered her thoughts about sitting on the sidelines, playing while everyone else was having a good time. Instead, it was the Bar Mitzvah boy's older sister, Rachel. The striking brunette seemed to be completely oblivious to her surroundings—and that included the music—as she gazed up into the face of the young man who was holding her to him so tightly.

As she looked on enviously, it appeared to Elizabeth that there didn't seem to be enough space between the two young people for a breath to sneak in—not even a shallow one. Anyone could see that they were lost in one another's eyes—and very much in love.

Elizabeth suppressed a sigh. Here was another occasion of her supplying the theme songs for someone else's life, someone else's romance. Without realizing it, the smile she'd kept fixed on her face slipped a little and a small frown took its place.

When was it her turn? she wondered in another moment of self-pity. When did she get to be swept up in her *own* romance?

"Everything okay, Lizzie?" Jack Borman whispered between barely moving lips as he leaned over toward her.

Jack was playing the portable keyboard he brought to all their mutual engagements. It was because of her previous association with Jack, whom she'd met while still in college, that she had gotten this particular gig, as well as a number of other engagements over the past few years.

Networking was all part of the life of a musician. If you managed to make enough acquaintances in this business, you hopefully got to play—and eat—on a fairly regular basis.

Elizabeth disliked being called Lizzie by some people and she knew that Jack was aware of that, but for some reason, calling her by that nickname seemed to amuse him. Since Jack was the source of a decent amount of work lately—and they *were* friends—she wasn't about to belabor the point that being referred to as "Lizzie" made her feel as if she were ten years old.

That it was also, coincidentally, the name of one of

her neighbor's cats—a calico cat that was undoubtedly the fattest feline she'd ever seen outside of a documentary on the Discovery Channel—made the name even less desirable to her.

Elizabeth leaned ever so slightly closer to Jack and his keyboard. "I'm just fine," she murmured, hoping that he'd leave it there.

But when their eyes met, she realized that she should have known better. Jack liked to think of himself as a minor deity, fixing things that had gone wrong in the lives of "his people," as he referred to the folks he kept on his roster of potential musicians to call whenever the need for a small orchestra came up.

Of all the musicians Jack had amassed to call for the various affairs he was contracted to play, he'd sent the most amount of work her way. It was no secret that he was interested in her for more than the way she handled a bow.

His interest had a definite social aspect to it, but so far, Elizabeth had managed to get out of accepting his various invitations to "unwind" after a performance—or the handful of rehearsals that preceded those performances.

His bushy eyebrows drew together over his hawk-like nose as he scrutinized her closely. "You don't look fine," he informed her.

"Must be the lighting," she murmured, doing her best to terminate the conversation.

Served her right for letting her thoughts get the better of her, Elizabeth upbraided herself. She was here to play—and pay her rent—not to wax envious at what it appeared others had that she did not.

For all she knew, what she thought she was witnessing could be strictly an illusion as well. Maybe this couple wouldn't even be together this time next year.

If that did turn out to be the case, she certainly didn't envy either of them the breakup that might be looming on the horizon.

A breakup, she thought, that would inevitably be filled with heartache if either one of them actually loved the other even half as much as appearances would indicate.

Enough already, Elizabeth silently chided herself. *What's* wrong *with me, anyway?*

She *knew* she was living her dreams. She had to cherish that and stop dwelling on what she didn't have. When had she gotten so negative?

Besides, careful what you wish for, remember?

With effort, Elizabeth drew her attention away from the romantic couple and closed her eyes, looking as if she were losing herself in her music.

What she was actually doing was protecting herself from making any further eye contact with Jack. She knew that in turn would leave the door open for him to make suggestions as to how to "put a smile on your face" as he liked to put it.

While she was grateful to Jack for the jobs, she would have been far happier just chalking it up to mere friendship. After all, if she were playing in an orchestra or ensemble that found itself needing a pianist, he would be the one she'd recommend.

But she had the uncomfortable feeling that he was actually sending gainful employment her way in a thinly veiled attempt at seducing her.

Eventually, she knew she was going to have to face up to telling him that there was absolutely no chemistry between them, that there was more chemistry between Columbus and the Native Americans when he landed on the shores of the New World than there was between Jack and her.

Elizabeth bit her lower lip, knowing that time was coming sooner than later.

Her eyes flew open as she heard Jack whisper, "I'm having a little party of my own after this shindig. If you're interested..." he added meaningfully.

She upped the wattage of her smile—one of her best features according to her father—and said, "I'd really love to—"

Jack looked startled, but managed to recover quickly. "Great, I'll—"

"—but I can't," Elizabeth continued in very hushed tones so as not to interfere with the music. "I've got to get ready for my studio gig in the morning. It's for an episode of *More than Roommates*."

The name of the popular sitcom evidently meant nothing to Jack since he didn't watch episodic television. He frowned over his apparent strike-out. Again.

"That's tomorrow?" he asked vaguely.

Elizabeth nodded, concentrating harder, determined not to miss a single beat. "That's right."

Jack grew silent for a moment. He was devoted to his craft, but he also clearly had designs on being more than just a fellow musician in Elizabeth's eyes.

"Blow it off," he told her suddenly. "I can get you another studio gig with—"

She cut him off with a slight, although emphatic,

shake of the head. "I already agreed to it. You're only as good as your word in this business," she reminded him as tactfully as she could. Jack had it in him to be a really good friend and she didn't want to hurt his feelings, but she didn't like having her back to the wall this way, either.

Jack shrugged, his thin shoulders rising and falling rather hard beneath his tuxedo as he muttered, "Your loss."

The way Elizabeth said "I know" helped assuage his wounded ego just as she'd intended. She could see it in his expression as he pulled himself away from the carefully couched rejection.

Maybe eventually they'd work this thing out, she thought. At least she could hope.

Elizabeth threw herself into the next number and tried to put this unpleasant episode behind her.

Her apartment felt lonelier than usual as Elizabeth let herself in later that evening.

She'd deliberately left a light on when she'd departed earlier for the Bar Mitzvah, anticipating that she just might need help in being upbeat when she came home.

Unfortunately, the light didn't manage to do the trick—that aching loneliness was still waiting for her.

Or rather, it had ridden home with her in the car, growing more and more acute with every mile that brought her closer to her empty apartment.

Locking the door behind her, she threw her keys and purse onto the top of the small bookcase near the door and stepped out of her shoes.

Maybe she needed a pet, Elizabeth mused. A warm,

happy puppy to jump up and greet her as she came through the door.

For a split second, she actually considered it. She certainly had an abundance of love to give to a pet. But then she thought of how guilty she'd feel about keeping the poor thing cooped up in the apartment while she was away at work. Considering how sporadic and unstructured her engagements were, the puppy wouldn't be able to have anything that resembled a normal, regular schedule.

Besides, she reminded herself, Mrs. Goldberg had Lizzie and she was forever telling her how lonely she was for actual company ever since "her Albert" had passed on. The feline, while fairly affectionate, still didn't fill the gap she had in her heart, the older woman had confessed sadly.

No, the cure for this loneliness that kept wrapping its tentacles around her lately was just more work, Elizabeth decided. It was while she was playing that she felt whole, as if she was contributing something worthwhile and beautiful to the universe. The violin was capable of making its audience both laugh and weep, and she could make it do both with aplomb.

Elizabeth glanced at the answering machine as she walked past it. The red light was blinking, telling her she had messages.

One, she knew, was bound to be from her father. That wonderful man always called her every night, no matter how busy his day had been, just to check in on her.

Now there's something to really be grateful for, she told herself. Not everyone had a father like that, a man who had single-handedly raised her and her two younger brothers while he was juggling a full-time career as a physician.

With very little warning, he'd been blindsided by his wife's sudden onset of pancreatic cancer and just like that, he'd found himself a widower with three young children.

Rather than farming his kids off to a female relative, or gladly abdicating his role to some full-time nanny he paid to raise his children, he'd painstakingly rearranged his life so that he could be there for every school play, every concert, even every parent/teacher conference. Elizabeth would forever be grateful to her dad for all the sacrifices he'd made over the years. There wasn't anything that she wouldn't do for him—and she knew her brothers felt the same way.

Maybe that was part of why she was having such trouble finding someone to share her life with, Elizabeth thought. She wanted to meet a man who had the warmth, the integrity, the sensitivity that her father had. She supposed that her standards were just too high.

But then, her father met those standards. So wasn't it reasonable to believe that there might be someone else in the world like that? Someone who, in addition to all the aforementioned attributes, could also make her world stand still.

That was how, she remembered, her mother had told her that she'd felt the very first time that she'd met her father.

It was one of Elizabeth's most cherished memories, sitting beside her mother, flipping through an album of old photographs. She remembered it was raining that day. She had to have been around four or five. Eric had been around two, and Ethan was still in his crib. She and her mother had looked over the album for hours. Her mother had a story about every photograph.

The next summer, her mother was gone.

Just like that.

A victim of an insidious, cruel disease. It had taken her father nearly two years to forgive himself for not being able to save her.

That was real love, she thought.

And that was what she was never destined to find for herself. Elizabeth pressed her lips together. She was just going to have to make her peace with that—if she was ever to have any peace at all.

Besides, she thought, how would she feel if she finally found that one special someone and then lost him, the way her father had lost her mother? Maybe it was for the best to just avoid the pain altogether.

With a resigned sigh she went to the refrigerator to see what she had that might lend itself to at least partially filling the emptiness she felt in her stomach.

There wasn't much to choose from.

Her father always sent her home with food whenever she visited him. In addition to being a top-notch physician, her father was also a terrific cook who could throw together sumptuous meals out of next to nothing.

She, however, lacked the cooking gene that thrived so well in his veins. Despite the fact that her brothers both knew how to whip things up, her father had failed to pass that particular trait on to her in any manner, shape or form.

She burned water when she boiled it.

Consequently, the only items that resided in her refrigerator after she ran out of the home-cooked meals her father loaded her down with were leftovers from the local take-out restaurants.

She took a quick survey—not that there was all that much to look over.

"Leftover Chinese it is," Elizabeth murmured, pulling out a couple of cartons with red Chinese characters embossed on the sides.

She brought the cartons over to the small dinette table she had set up in the alcove. Taking the portable phone receiver over with her as well, Elizabeth made herself comfortable. She took a few bites of food—she wasn't altogether clear on exactly what she was eating at this point since the meals all tended to blend together after a couple of days—and pressed Play.

The first call, as she'd guessed, was from her father. Elizabeth smiled as she listened.

"Are you there, Elizabeth?" There was a slight pause as he waited for a pickup. "No? Guess you're busy playing. I know, old joke. But I still like it. Old has its place, you know. Like your old dad."

"You're not old, Dad," she murmured affectionately. "You're distinguished."

"Hope it was a good evening for you," her father continued. "Sorry I didn't get to talk to you in person. Nothing new on this end. One of your brothers is working, the other one isn't." A slight chuckle accompanied the statement. "Two out of three isn't bad, I always say. Sleep well, my virtuoso. I'll try to catch you tomorrow. If not, see you on Thursday. Love you." It was the way her father ended every phone call to her, the way he sent her off each time they parted company. Hearing it always made her smile—and feel safe.

"Love you, too, Dad," Elizabeth said softly to the machine.

Just the sound of her father's deep, authoritative voice somehow managed to make her feel better, she thought as she pressed for the next message.

Ten seconds into the call, she pressed the button to bypass the message. It was someone asking for a contribution to some college on the East Coast that she had never heard of.

The third and last message was the kind of message that she listened for, the ones that involved her bread and butter.

The deep, resonant voice caught her attention immediately. Putting down her fork, she picked up a pen, drew her pad to her and listened for details.

"I'm not sure if I have the right number, but a Mrs. Manetti suggested I call. She's catering for me. Well, not me, but my parents, except they don't know—" She heard the man sigh, as if annoyed with the way that had come out. "Let me start over," he said.

"Go right ahead," Elizabeth murmured, amused. She popped a quick forkful into her mouth, picked up her pen again and waited.

"I'm hosting this special party and someone suggested that music would be good—"

"Yes," Elizabeth said to the phone, heartily agreeing. "Music is always good."

And so was getting paid for making it, she thought fondly.

The man with the deep voice cleared his throat several times, and she waited patiently for the message to continue.

"I'll…uh…try to get you later," he finally said just before terminating the call.

That's it? Elizabeth stared accusingly at her answering machine.

"I can't believe he just hung up," she said incredulously. She pressed the button that allowed her to look at the previous call, wanting to find the man's phone number via the caller ID feature since he hadn't left it on the garbled, aborted message.

The word *private* spread out across the small screen. Using the *69 feature on her phone yielded the same frustrating results. No phone number, no name, no nothing. The man with the sultry voice and the tied tongue obviously valued his privacy.

Elizabeth blew out an exasperated breath. Nothing she hated more than to think she was going to be offered a job only to have it reneged.

Or, in this case, dangled before her, and then pulled like some carrot on a string.

Maybe he'll call back, she thought, putting the receiver back down. All she could do was hope. She wasn't at a place in her life where she could just shrug carelessly when it came to the promise of money. She needed every gig she could line up.

"Maybe tomorrow will be better," she murmured to herself.

She erased message number two and three, clearing space on her machine for more messages. If Mr. Sultry Voice didn't call back, someone else would. Happily, someone always did. After all her monthly bills were taken care of, she'd put the remainder of whatever money she'd earned aside in what amounted to a tiny nest egg. She turned to the latter on those occasions when she found herself needing to bridge the financial gap between engagements.

Lucky for her that her needs were few and her tastes were the exact opposite of extravagant, she thought, making short work of the leftover Chinese food.

Chapter Two

"So, how did it go, Jared? Were you able to reach Elizabeth to make the arrangements?" Theresa Manetti's melodic voice asked early the next morning when, bleary-eyed and semiconscious, he'd managed to pick up the phone receiver on his second attempt.

The caterer had caught Jared Winterset completely off guard. He'd been up late, working on an ad campaign that needed some serious last-minute revamping and fueling his flagging energy with bracing black coffee, which could have walked off on its own power at any time. Consequently, he wasn't firing on all four cylinders this morning when he answered his phone.

Jared liked the woman. His path had crossed Mrs. Manetti's because, in his line of work, he occasionally had to throw a few parties for his clients. Someone had given him her card a couple of years ago, along with a glowing recommendation that turned out to be right on the money. Theresa took pride in her work and had a personal stake in every affair she catered. The food, he could honestly say, was incredible.

Over time, they struck up an easy friendship. She was like the doting aunt he'd never had and he valued her input. It was Theresa who had given him the name and phone number of the violinist he hadn't been able to reach last night.

He wondered now if possibly the two were related. Why else would Theresa be calling at this hour to find out how it went?

"No," he answered. "She wasn't home. I tried to leave a message on her answering machine, but that didn't work out too well."

Rather than just letting it go at that, Theresa surprised him by wanting to know, "What happened?"

For the second time in two minutes, she'd caught him off guard.

"Bad connection," he answered. Okay, so it was a lie, he thought, but he really didn't feel like going into the fact that he'd hung up midmessage after becoming tongue-tied and unable to articulate even the simplest of thoughts.

Instead of making a second attempt at leaving a coherent voice mail, Jared had decided to just try again another time. His hopes were that the future call would get him in contact with a human being rather than an irritating recording announcing that no one could take his call at the moment, but to please leave a message after the tone.

The sad truth was that answering machines left him somewhat disoriented, and if not exactly flustered, certainly not at the top of his game. After all, he was an ad executive who had great people skills according to his annual evaluations at the firm, not to mention the input given to his superiors by very satisfied clients. But, despite all that, there was no getting away from the fact that he just didn't feel right talking to a machine—in this case, the answering machine.

Jared would have been the first to admit that inanimate objects held no interest for him. That was the main reason why, other than when the necessity for extensive research arose, he spent next to no time online. He had no overwhelming desire to look up old acquaintances or strike up new friendships via the internet.

He was and had always been a one-on-one kind of a guy and he liked it that way just fine. It was what made him so good at ad campaigns. He made them seem as if they were speaking solely to each person in the audience.

"But you'll try getting in touch with her again?" The way Theresa asked the question, it was as if his answer was a foregone conclusion.

"Well, I'm going to be kind of busy for the next few days," he told her. There were still a great many details about the celebration to iron out, not to mention that he had several clients' hands to hold through a rough time. "I've got an idea," he told Theresa. "Why don't you just make the arrangements for a band for me?" he suggested. "I mean, you're already handling the catering and you've always done a bang-up job with that."

No, no! You're not getting the point, Theresa thought in frustration. Frustration she managed to completely hide from the intended target of all this effort.

Maizie, one of her two dearest friends in the whole world, had called her the moment she'd left the doctor's office, telling her about Dr. Stephens's daughter. Maizie had put both her and Cecilia, her other friend, on high alert. Between the three of them, she was certain that they could find someone for Dr. Stephens's daughter.

Theresa had gotten lucky first. But nothing ever went smoothly, she thought now.

"I'll do anything you want me to with food, Jared, but I think that you should be the one to select your parents' music," she suggested tactfully. "After all, you're the one who knows what they like—"

Actually, he didn't have a clue as to what his parents liked to listen to. He vaguely remembered that when he was a child, his mother used to like to play old show tunes—but he didn't know if she still did—and as for his father… Off the top of his head, he couldn't recall if the old man favored one style of music over another.

"Probably the same thing you like" was his best guess.

This wasn't going to be as easy as their last effort to pair up a couple, Theresa thought. But she was nothing if not a study in quiet determination. People, it was her firm belief, were much happier in pairs than alone.

"Be that as it may, Jared. I know that I would be touched if my son was personally involved in *all* the preparations for my thirty-fifth wedding anniversary. Trust me, mothers are funny like that," she added as her closing argument.

Before he could jump in with another rebuttal, an idea came to her. "I happen to know that Ms. Stephens will be playing at Paragon Studios today. She's part of a small ensemble recording the background music for this romantic-comedy series, *More than Roommates*. Why don't you drop by and give her a listen?" She paused. "That way you can hear her perform in person and that'll help you make up your mind about the pluses of having live music at your parents' party."

It sounded reasonable, but there was one thing wrong with her suggestion. "I can't just waltz onto a sound-stage," Jared pointed out. He didn't know all that much about the mechanics of taping a show, but he did know that.

If he thought this was over, he was mistaken, Theresa thought with a tinge of triumph.

"Not most studios," she agreed. "But you can this one. The director's an old friend of mine. I'll give him a call and I know he won't mind you coming in—as long as you just observe."

The woman had an answer for everything. Jared felt as if he'd just gotten in the path of a hurricane and been swept up. He laughed, surrendering. "Fine, you get the okay, and I'll go listen—but it'll have to be in the late afternoon," he stipulated. "I have to be in the office today."

"No problem. These things run over," Theresa assured him, recalling what little she did know about tapings. "I'll call you back with details," she promised.

He shook his head as he hung up. Maybe the woman was right. He'd hired Theresa on a number of occasions, and he fully respected both her work ethic and her opinion. Besides, she was around his parents' age. She would know better than he what would please them. They'd probably like having a live band.

He smiled to himself. This was something his sister, Megan, hadn't thought of when she left him with a list of things to follow up on—just before she went off on that extended cruise with her husband.

Megan was going to be surprised at his intuitiveness, he thought. She didn't have to know that the suggestion had come from the caterer.

However, he had no way of knowing that Theresa and her friends, Maizie and Cecilia, had banded together to form a matchmaking group that had been dubbed "Matchmaking Mamas" by one of their children. All three women were successful businesswomen in their own right, but making matches for their children and their friends' children was where their hearts really lay.

And so far, they had a perfect record.

Theresa had no intention of having that streak be broken.

The friend Theresa called the moment she hung up with Jared wasn't the director she'd mentioned—it was Cecilia, her other dear friend and comrade-in-arms. Cecilia was the one who knew the director on the sitcom. The company Cecilia owned provided cleaning services, and she personally oversaw the cleaning of the director's sprawling mansion twice a month.

Favors were called in and within twenty minutes, all arrangements were made. Jared would be allowed onto the set for the taping.

Theresa called back and cheerfully informed her young client that "All systems are a go, Jared."

"Excuse me?" Preoccupied with the account that had kept him up, he wasn't sure what the woman was referring to. Juggling his phone as well as his house keys, he was trying to shrug into his jacket as he made his way out the door.

Theresa patiently spelled it out. "Ted Riley, the director of *More than Roommates,* said you could come onto the set anytime after four today. That's when they're taping the final take of the background music for the episode."

One arm punched through a sleeve, Jared stopped putting on his jacket, and glanced at his watch. He had a meeting with a client at noon. With any luck, it would be wrapped up by four. That meant he'd be free to drive over to Paragon Studios. If he recalled his geography, Paragon Studios was only approximately two miles away from his client's offices.

"Okay, since you've gone through all this trouble, I'll swing by and give that woman a listen." And then he laughed as he put his arm through the second sleeve. "You do know that you should join the U.N. and use your powers of persuasion for good, don't you, Theresa?"

Tickled, she laughed lightly and said, "That's exactly what I am doing, Jared. I'm using my 'powers' for the greater good." *Your good—and Elizabeth's,* she added silently.

Jared didn't question her any further. He just assumed the woman was referring to helping him with the arrangements for his parents' celebration.

Elizabeth shifted ever so slightly. She could feel the handsome stranger's eyes on her.

She'd noticed him immediately, although he'd obviously tried to be unobtrusive when he'd slipped onto the set ten minutes ago. He'd stood off to the side as gaffers, cameramen and other technical pros scurried about, just barely managing to keep clear of the very small area where the ensemble was playing.

He'd tried to go unnoticed, but a man who looked like that wasn't the kind who exactly blended into the scenery. Tall, with straight black hair and near-perfect angular features, not to mention wide shoulders and a trim waist with slim hips, he looked as if he should have been in front of the camera, not off to one side behind it.

Why was this dashing gentleman watching her play so intently? Was her fingering off? Or was there something wrong with the way she was dressed?

But even as the questions occurred to her, she knew that the answer to each was no. She was wearing the same kind of attire that the other musicians had on, and her fingering hadn't been off since she was five.

Was he another technical adviser? Someone associated with the studio who wanted to make sure that money wasn't being wasted on musicians who couldn't hold a note?

She knew that a lot of the music for programs these days was of the prerecorded variety, just artfully melded by one person in a sound booth to avoid the expense of having a six-piece ensemble supply live play.

"And—it's a wrap," the director finally declared. Vibrant just a few seconds ago, he looked weary now and incredibly relieved to be wrapping up a shoot that had taken longer than he'd anticipated.

"Thank you, people. You can go home now," he announced, waving them off the set.

The moment she started packing up her instrument and the sheet music, the handsome observer began to make his way toward her.

"Excuse me." The deep, resonant voice was polite as he tried to get her attention.

The moment he opened his mouth, she was struck by a feeling of déjà vu. That voice was familiar. Where had she heard it before? Elizabeth wondered.

But the next moment, she nixed the thought. How could his voice sound familiar? She'd never met the man. She definitely would have remembered meeting someone who looked like him.

Still, she couldn't shake the feeling that she'd heard his voice somewhere before. On a commercial perhaps? Elizabeth stopped packing up her violin in its case and gave him her undivided attention.

"Yes?"

Theresa hadn't mentioned that the woman was a knockout as well as talented. He found he had to struggle to maintain his train of thought. "Are you Elizabeth Stephens?"

Definitely a familiar voice, she thought. But where had she—?

"Yes," she answered, her curiosity piqued.

Jared decided to treat this like an ad campaign and plunged right in. "Theresa Manetti suggested that I get in contact with you."

Elizabeth shook her head. She had no idea who he was referring to. It certainly wasn't the name of someone who had hired her to play before. She had each and every client's name and number memorized.

Raising her head, Elizabeth looked the man straight

in the eyes—noting that they were a knee-numbing light green.

"I'm afraid I don't know who that is," she told him.

He had to have her confused with someone else, she decided—then immediately backtracked. The man knew her name, so he *couldn't* have her confused with someone else. But who was this Theresa Manetti, and why was she sending this man to her?

"Really?" Jared asked, somewhat confused himself. "She speaks very highly of you."

And then it hit her—why his voice sounded so familiar. It was the same voice she'd heard stumbling on her answering machine last night. He was the incomplete call that had abruptly ended in midsentence.

Her eyes pinned him in place, daring him to deny what she was about to say. "You called me last night."

Instead of denying it, he surprised her by owning up to the botched call. "I did."

"But you hung up," she pointed out.

He looked slightly chagrined, like a kid caught with his hand in the cookie jar and unable to pull it out, or even come up with a plausible reason why his hand was there in the first place.

"Sorry about that," he apologized.

Face-to-face, he could easily make up an excuse as to why he'd terminated the call. Power failure, a dropped signal—there were myriad reasons for him to choose from. But he didn't see the advantage of beginning what would only be a very short association—his parents' anniversary was in three and a half weeks— with lies and excuses.

So he told her the truth. "I'm not very good when it comes to talking to answering machines," he confessed.

"I noticed," she acknowledged, then laughed softly. "Just between you and me, I've got the same problem. If you call in person, I can guarantee that I pretty much could talk your ear off. But if I find myself on the other end of some robotic-sounding recorder, I go completely blank."

Her summation of the problem amused him. "Nice to know I'm not alone." He became aware that the director was looking expectantly in his direction. "I think we're in the way here," Jared said.

Now that he'd met her, he wasn't so keen on pulling the plug on the music anymore. He looked around the soundstage, but there didn't even seem to be the hint of a vending machine around.

He looked at her. "Is there somewhere we can go where we can talk?"

Though she told herself she was letting her imagination run away with her, Elizabeth felt her pulse kick into high gear.

She inwardly chided herself for getting carried away. The man obviously meant he just wanted to talk to her about her playing abilities, not because he was as drawn to her as she was to him. Someone who looked the way this man did was either married, spoken for or extremely busy socially.

"Well, you could walk me to my car," she suggested. "Other than that, I think there's a coffee shop about a block away outside the gates," she told him, trying to picture the place.

He glanced at his watch. He just wanted to make

sure that he didn't lose track of time. He had an early meeting tomorrow and he needed to have some rough drafts of the new campaign for Getaway Resorts done before then.

"Ordinarily, coffee would sound great, but I've already had twice my quota today…and if I have any more, there's no way I'm going to get any sleep tonight. Maybe I should just walk you to your car."

She nodded, surprised at the sliver of disappointment that seemed to slice through her. She told herself she was behaving like an adolescent, but somehow, that didn't seem to change her feelings.

"Walking it is," she declared dramatically, then lowered her voice as if she were part of a stage performance. "Although I should warn you, I didn't exactly park close."

Elizabeth led the way out of the soundstage, taking a side door marked Exit.

The darkness enveloped them the moment they came out.

"As a matter of fact," she went on to say, "if you didn't have time to get in your morning run today, this will probably make up for it—and then some."

Her comment bemused him. "What makes you think I run?"

She looked at him as if the question didn't even really require an answer. "This is Southern California. Everyone always claims to be into all kinds of exercise out here. Running was the first thing that came to mind."

Also, a body like yours doesn't come from a mail-order catalog, she added silently. He made her think of Michelangelo's *David*—except more so.

"Do you?" she asked out loud. When he looked at her somewhat quizzically, she added, "Run?"

"Only when I'm late getting somewhere and the car doesn't work," he quipped. He had no idea what made him share the next piece of information with her. "I've got an elliptical trainer in the garage that guilts me out every night when I park my car inside."

"That's simple enough to avoid," she told him, then suggested, "You could try parking your car in the driveway instead."

He saw the twinkle in her eyes, and laughed. He liked her sense of humor. "Sounds like a plan," he murmured.

As the sound of his laugh wrapped itself around her, Elizabeth caught herself returning his smile.

Chapter Three

"So," Jared said once they stepped outside Paragon Studios, "where's your car?"

"You can't see it from here, but it's that way," Elizabeth told him, pointing in the general direction. "We're going to have to walk a little bit before you can see it."

Jared shook his head. He'd thought she was exaggerating before. Obviously not. "You weren't kidding about your car being parked far away."

She stopped and looked at him. Taking the man on a forced march was *not* the way to win over a potential employer. "If it's too far for you, you really don't have to walk me to my car."

He laughed and waved away her words. "Just an observation, Ms. Stephens, not a complaint. The way I look at it, the exercise will do me good." They resumed walking, stopping only to get out of the way of a car that was pulling out. "But seriously, why did you park so far away from the actual soundstage?"

Most of the people he knew tried to find a space that was close to their destination, not park in the next county.

"The first time I came here, I found that the parking spaces that were near the building were either reserved, or already taken. I didn't want to waste time driving up and down the aisles, looking for someplace that was relatively close, so I just took the first space I saw when I pulled in."

Megan could stand to learn a lot from this woman. "I bet you get a lot more Christmas shopping done with that philosophy," Jared speculated. His sister spent half her time cruising the lots, looking for that one perfect spot that just happened to be right in front of the mall entrance.

"I don't know about my philosophy having anything to do with it, but I'm usually done with Christmas shopping in November." Glancing over at him, she noted that Jared looked as stunned as if she'd just told him she had superpowers.

"You're kidding," he said incredulously. "November? Really?"

She nodded. "That's right," she confirmed, then decided that maybe an explanation was in order. "That way, I can take my time, and then enjoy the season instead of dashing madly about, looking for some picked-over last-minute gifts that people may or may not like." But there was also a more practical reason for her spreading out her shopping season. "Besides, December is one of my busiest months. People seem to like violin music more when there's a Christmas tree involved."

Her phraseology amused him, but he pretended to take her comment seriously. "Must be the smell of pine," he quipped.

Elizabeth nodded, mimicking his overall tone. "Must be."

He liked the way her mouth curved ever so slightly as she was trying to keep a straight face. Liked the smile in her brilliant blue eyes. Since they had a ways to go before they reached her car, Jared decided to use that time to find out a few things about this attractive blonde.

He started with an easy question. "How long have you been playing the violin?" he asked her.

She knew the exact moment she had started playing in earnest, but for simplicity—and because the story wasn't one she shared with someone she'd just met—she said flippantly, "Sometimes it feels as if I were born clutching a violin in my hands."

"Must have been a really rough delivery for your poor mother," he deadpanned.

The mention of her mother—even in jest the way this obviously was intended—always brought a sliver of pain piercing her heart.

Though her mother was gone by the time she had entered kindergarten, Elizabeth had a handful of memories that she treasured and hung on to for dear life. One of those memories involved listening to her mother playing the violin for her father.

It was shortly after her mother's death, in an effort to try to cheer her father up, that she picked up her mother's violin and began to play it. She managed to miraculously recall the way her mother had stroked the bow over the strings while fingering them. What resulted might not have been ready to be heard in any concert hall, but at least it didn't sound as if she was scraping her nails against a chalkboard.

Immensely touched and even more impressed, her father signed her up for violin lessons the very next day. To that end, he also gave her mother's violin to her to use during her lessons.

Elizabeth could remember regarding the violin nervously. To attempt to play it once in order to cheer up her father was one thing, to suddenly become the keeper of this precious instrument was quite another. And quite a responsibility.

She recalled looking up at her father and asking, "Daddy, are you sure?"

"Very sure," he'd told her firmly, then added the words that completely won her over. "Your mother would have wanted you to have it."

Entrusted with this sacred duty, Elizabeth had taken loving care of it, taking great pains to keep the violin in top playing condition. When it finally had to be re-strung, she retained the original strings, putting them carefully into an envelope and tucking the envelope away in her jewelry box, something else that she'd inherited from her mother.

Jared noticed the serious expression that had crossed her face. Noticed, too, that she had suddenly become very quiet.

"I'm sorry," he apologized, thinking this sudden

change in her attitude was his fault. "Did I say something wrong?"

Elizabeth shook her head. He had nothing to do with the thoughts that were going through her head. Her mother had been gone for twenty-one years, but there were times that it felt like only yesterday.

"No," she told him softly. "I was just thinking." That was an open-ended sentence, begging for more of an explanation, and she knew it. But for the moment, she didn't feel like going into it. She had no desire to either unload, or to make him feel uncomfortable and guilty for raising the subject of her mother, however innocently, since she had passed on.

"About…?" he prodded.

"Nothing of importance," she finally said. "This violin belonged to my mother, and I was just worried that I might have nicked it earlier," she lied. "I'm sorry, you probably think I'm obsessing."

"Not at all. Perfectly normal to want to take care of a beautiful thing," he said.

He was being kind, she thought, finding herself more and more drawn to this handsome, likable man.

"Your mother used to play?" he asked her.

Elizabeth felt pride swelling within her. "Like an angel."

But even as she said it, it occurred to Elizabeth that she was spending too much time talking about her personal life. While friendly, she didn't usually open up this much about herself. It was definitely time to change topics.

"So, what's the occasion?" she asked him brightly.

She'd switched gears a bit too fast, she realized when

he looked at her quizzically and asked, "What do you mean?"

"I'm assuming that you don't want to hire me to serenade you outside your bedroom window. So, what's the occasion?" she repeated.

For just a second, Jared allowed himself to dwell on the scenario she'd just drawn for him. The very idea of her playing her violin just for him outside his window both amused him and—in an odd sort of way—aroused him.

He realized he was letting his mind wander while she was waiting for a response. "My parents' thirty-fifth wedding anniversary is coming up in a little more than three weeks. Why, does that make a difference?"

"Absolutely. The occasion always makes a difference," she told him. "There's a different mind-set involved in playing for a couple who've been together for thirty-five years than, say, playing at a wedding where the couple is just starting out. And both require different preparations than setting up to play at a high school graduation party."

"Get to play for many of those?" he asked, amused. When he'd graduated high school, he'd hung out all night celebrating with his friends. He didn't even remember he *had* parents until the following morning.

"You'd be surprised at how many indulgent parents live in Beverly Hills," she answered. And then a question hit her. "Was that my audition?" she asked, seemingly out of the blue. "Back there, in the studio," she clarified, nodding back toward the building now in the distance.

It was starting to make sense. "You really should

signal when you're switching lanes like that. Otherwise, a person could get whiplash," he said drily. "As for your question, I don't know if I'd call it an audition, but the woman who gave me your name thought it might be a good thing to hear you in action, so to speak. I liked what I heard," he was quick to add. "I should have realized that I would since Theresa speaks so highly of you."

There was that name again, she thought. Who was he talking about?

"Theresa," Elizabeth repeated, her tone all but inviting him to add a surname to the woman's given one.

But when he did, she was no more enlightened than she'd been before. "Theresa Manetti."

Elizabeth did a quick mental run through her client list. The woman's last name didn't ring any bells. As far as she knew, she'd never dealt with a Theresa Manetti when it came to making arrangements to play at a party or a gig.

Moving over to one side in order to avoid stepping on a rather fat wad of bubble gum, she shook her head. "I'm sorry, I just don't remember this woman."

He thought that odd but pressed on. "She was the one who told me where you'd be working this morning and set it up so that I could come down and hear you play for myself." He shrugged. "Actually, although she didn't say it in so many words, I got the feeling that she really wanted me to meet you as soon as possible."

"Huh," Elizabeth murmured to herself. She still wasn't getting an image in her head. "Did this Theresa Manetti happen to tell you where she heard me play? I'm pretty good about remembering the people who hire me, so I'm guessing she might have heard me at one of the little theater groups in the area."

For all she knew, the woman could have just been part of one of the audiences, but if that were the case, how did this Manetti woman know her name or her schedule? This wasn't making any sense to her.

Jared, meanwhile, had been sidetracked by something she'd just said. "You play for theater groups, too?"

She wasn't sure if he was impressed, or just surprised. In either case, the answer to his question was the same.

"Yes."

He was undoubtedly wondering why she didn't stick to a single venue. Aside from variety being the spice of life, there was a far more basic reason behind her working all these diverse jobs.

"It takes a lot of gigs to stitch together a living," she told him honestly. "Unless you're a world-class musician who can pretty much write your own ticket, you have to scramble to find work anywhere you can. And I really do love show music," she confided. "As a matter of fact, I'm playing at the Bedford Theater this weekend. They're doing *Fiddler on the Roof.* It's their final weekend," she informed him. "I can leave you a ticket at the box office for this Sunday if you'd like to come."

He didn't want to inconvenience her, or ask for special treatment. "You don't have to do that," he protested.

She laughed at his protest. "Are you kidding? The more bodies, the better. It's a known fact. Musicians always play better to a packed house," she said with a wink.

He found the wink incredibly appealing, not to mention sexy. Without realizing it, he glanced down at her hand to see if there was a promise ring, or an engagement ring or, worse yet, a wedding ring on the appropriate finger. When he saw that there wasn't—and there was no telltale pale line there to indicate a recent removal of said ring—he smiled broadly at her.

"Then I'll definitely make it a point to catch the show," he promised. "Thanks for the ticket."

"Hey, my pleasure," she responded with sincerity before suddenly realizing that she hadn't been paying the strictest attention while they were walking. They were practically on top of her car and she hadn't noticed. A few more steps and they would have overshot it. If she had, she was certain he would have thought he was hiring an idiot to play for his parents' big day.

"We're here," she announced belatedly, gesturing toward her vehicle.

Jared stopped walking and looked around, scanning the area. This really was the end of the lot, he thought. For the most part, it was almost empty. Except for what looked like old T-bird, the initial model, which had been all but pocket-size when it came out.

"Is that your car?" he asked incredulously.

She couldn't even begin to guess what was going through the man's head, except that she was certain that at least a part of him was undoubtedly thinking that a car like that was wasted on a woman.

"That's my car," she said proudly.

He knew that the car was regarded as vintage, but all that meant to him was that it was old. "Let me guess," he mused, peering at the vehicle from several different angles. He gave no clue as to what he was looking for. "That belonged to your mother, too, right?"

She supposed that her beloved car did look old enough to be considered a hand-me-down from one generation to the next.

"No," she told him. "That's the first thing I bought with my earnings as a violinist. I saved up for six months for it," she said, remembering.

He heard the affection in her voice. Obviously Elizabeth saw something in the vehicle that he didn't, Jared thought. He tended to like new things rather than things that had weathered the passage of time. Those needed coddling and he didn't consider himself the type to do that. Everything in his life was kept on the light, uninvolved side, as per his plan.

"And it still runs?" he asked, surprised.

She grinned. "Most of the time," she allowed. There was no point in dwelling on the times that it hadn't. That was behind her now. "She does get temperamental every now and then," she added fondly, "but I can't stay mad at her. Lola always comes through in a pinch."

"Lola?"

"That's what I call my car. What do you call your car?" she wanted to know.

"Reliable," he answered, then commented on the logistics that were complicating her life. "Sounds like you were describing a grumpy old uncle a minute ago and not a car."

"It's a little bit of both," she confessed. "But nothing I can't handle, although I have to admit that the parts for Lola are getting harder and harder for me to find."

He made a tactful suggestion. "Has it ever occurred to you to buy a new car?"

She shook her head. "No. I don't abandon things just because they're getting on a little in age," she said with feeling. It was one of the main principles she lived by: she stuck with things.

Unlocking the door on the driver's side, Elizabeth deposited her violin into the backseat, then leaned in to slip open the glove compartment.

Standing behind her, Jared got a particularly good view of the backs of her shapely legs as her black skirt rode up on her thighs. She was reaching across both seats in order to get at the glove compartment.

Jared knew he shouldn't be staring, it wasn't right. But he had to admit that what he was being privy to was a very appealing sight.

Getting what she wanted, Elizabeth straightened up and snaked her way out of the vehicle. She found herself bumping up against Jared. When she looked at him questioningly, he muttered a semiexcuse.

"I thought you might need help taking something out of the car."

The look in her eyes told him that she didn't believe his alibi, and when she grinned, he could have sworn that he could literally *feel* the impression of her lips on his. The sensation drew out his smile in response.

"The card's not all that heavy," she told him.

"Card?" he repeated, lost.

"Card." She held it up for his perusal. It was a business card for the little theater group performing the musical this weekend. On it was the address, the box office hours and the theater's telephone number.

"The final performance is this Sunday," she repeated, in case he'd already forgotten. "Curtain goes up at seven," she added.

"I'll be there before seven," he promised. Closing his hand over the card, he slipped it into his pocket. "Looking forward to it."

He glanced at his watch out of habit. When Jared saw the time, he frowned. He was far behind schedule and they hadn't even gotten around to any of the specifics about the gig. "Look, can I call you later on tonight?" he wanted to know.

For just one isolated moment, she thought Jared was asking to call her on a social basis. But the next second, she knew that wasn't possible. After all, he'd done nothing to indicate that he would be interested in seeing Elizabeth the woman instead of Elizabeth the violinist.

"Absolutely," she told him with a bright smile. "I should be home for most of the evening."

"Good, then I won't get your answering machine again." He shrugged, ever so slightly self-conscious. "As I mentioned before…I'm not really too keen on talking to machines."

She laughed at the footnote he'd just tossed in her direction. He found the sound light, melodious and almost hypnotic.

"No worries… I'll be sure to pick up," she promised him, getting behind the wheel of her vintage car.

Jared stepped back, allowing her space to swing her door closed. "I'll talk to you then," he said.

Then, turning on his heel, he started retracing his steps to get to his own car, which was parked a good deal closer to the soundstage than Elizabeth's was.

The fact that he fully expected to hear her car start up but didn't had him stopping after about five steps and turning around.

He could see her frowning from where he stood. Frowning and going through the motions of starting her car up.

Still nothing.

Her beloved vintage car was apparently nonresponsive, no matter how many times she tried to get it to come back from the dead.

Chapter Four

Jared stood watching her for a moment longer, thinking that Elizabeth's car was just being temperamental. Some older models seemed to take their own sweet time starting up.

He was still waiting to hear her engine make the proper noises as he made his way back to the uncooperative Thunderbird.

"Problem?" he asked.

Elizabeth's frown deepened as she pumped the gas pedal one more time and turned her key. Still nothing. She was also afraid that she was going to wind up flooding the engine.

Frustrated, she sank back in her seat. "Not if I don't mind spending the night in the parking lot," she responded.

Moving to the front of her vehicle, Jared looked down at her headlights and said, "Turn on your lights."

She had no idea how that was going to help anything, but at this point she was willing to try anything. Shrugging, she did as he instructed.

"Now what?" she asked.

There wasn't so much as a glimmer in either headlight.

The phrase "dead as a doornail" came to mind as he frowned at the vehicle.

"Now nothing, I'm afraid," he told her. "Looks like your battery's dead."

Undaunted, she said hopefully, "Maybe we can jump it." She slid out from behind the wheel. "I've got jumper cables in my trunk."

Jared looked at her in surprise. He thought of that as being rather responsible for someone her age. He doubted if his sister even knew what jumper cables were. Experience taught you things like that.

"I take it this has happened before," he assumed.

She inclined her head and made a vague gesture he couldn't begin to interpret. "Once or twice. Or five," she muttered under her breath.

He still heard it. "All right, I'll go bring my car around and see what I can do."

But apparently, at least on the outset, he could do nothing—although it certainly wasn't for lack of trying.

Jared aligned his vehicle so that the two cars were literally nose to nose in the lot. Elizabeth took it from there. He was amazed at how expertly, not to mention quickly, she managed to hook up her car's battery to his.

"Start yours first," she urged as she got in behind the steering wheel in her car.

When the other engine hummed to life, Elizabeth pressed down on the gas pedal and turned the key, mentally crossing her fingers. She might as well not have bothered.

Her engine remained dormant.

There wasn't so much as a feeble whimper coming from that region. Every spark of life in the battery had been utterly siphoned off.

Jared came around to her side of the two tethered vehicles and looked down at her battery. Usually, when a mechanic swapped out a battery, he would scratch out the month and year on the new one to indicate just when it had been pressed into service. He saw nothing but spots of corrosion on top of this battery.

"How old is it?" he asked, tapping the top of the battery where the dates should have been.

"Old" was all she said. Then, because he was apparently waiting for more, she added, "I'm not really sure."

Jared tried another approach, hoping to jog her memory. "Have you put a new battery in since you bought the car?"

He saw a guilty look pass over her face in response to his question. A second later, she shook her head.

That answered that, he thought.

"Well," he began with a slight, drawn-out drawl, "the good news is I think we've located your problem."

Since he'd enunciated it like that, she braced herself before asking, "And the bad?"

"I'd say you definitely need a new battery, and most

auto parts places are probably closed for the night by now."

Fruitlessly trying to bring the battery around had taken them a while, and it was now after six.

Jared took out his smartphone and pressed a button to bring it back to life. The moment he did, his thumbs began to fly over the keyboard.

"Are you texting someone?" Actually, what she wanted to ask was *who* was he texting at a time like this.

It seemed to her a rather strange time to touch base with a friend. But then, on the other hand, why not? It was her car that had the problem, not his. He was perfectly free to do whatever he wanted, take off wherever he wanted.

"Just finding out if The Auto Mall is still open," he explained, referring to a popular auto parts chain. Still looking, he pulled up the chain's nearest location. The store hours were printed right underneath it. "It is," he announced.

Where was he going with this? she wondered. "Is that good?"

"Only if you want to drive home tonight," he told her glibly.

Taking a small notepad out of his other pocket, he jotted down the auto shop's address and then stood looking thoughtfully at his phone for a moment.

"Give me a minute," he told her. Turning his back on her, he hit one of the thirty preprogrammed numbers in his phone as he walked away.

Elizabeth watched him, wondering if he was calling a cab for her, or if the call even had anything to do with her dilemma.

Well, aren't you the swell-headed one?

Why should his call have anything to do with me?
Elizabeth asked herself. It wasn't as if the man was
obligated to help her. Her car would have gone dead
whether or not he had shown up today to catch her on-
air performance.

She just hoped that this little mishap hadn't cost her
a job. After all she was definitely not at her best with
this vehicle dead at her feet, and he might view her as
a flighty female who wasn't capable of staying on top
of the simplest of things…like regular maintenance
on her car.

In her defense, finding work these days was a full-
time job in itself. All the other details of her life—like
buying food or getting her car serviced—just had to
be fit around her search as best as she could manage.
Keeping tabs on the life of her battery, she thought ruefully as she glared at her nonresponsive vehicle, had
just fallen through the cracks.

And now, she thought, taking out her own phone,
she was paying for it.

She was about to call one of her brothers to ask for a
ride home when the handsome stranger sent her way by
the mysterious Theresa Manetti walked back up to her.

"All right," he told her, "we're all set."

"All set?" she echoed. Just how was being stranded
in a parking lot forty miles from home anything close
to that?

He shot her a reassuring look. "The manager said
he'd stay open for us, as long as we get there in the next
twenty minutes."

"Manager?" She was beginning to feel as if she'd

slipped into some parallel universe where she'd landed the role of the village idiot, destined to repeat words that made no sense to her in their present context. "Manager of what?" she wanted to know.

"Manager of the vintage parts section in The Auto Mall," he explained, then nodded toward his own car. "C'mon," he urged. "Get in."

Rather than comply, she remained where she was, trying to process what he was saying. "Wait, you're driving to The Auto Mall?"

"Well, I left my helicopter in my other jacket," he deadpanned, "so yes, I'm driving. The funny thing about batteries, they don't come when you call them so we're going to have to go and pick it up at the store."

Why was he doing this? He didn't even *know* her. And then something else struck her. "Didn't you say you had a schedule to keep, or an appointment to go to?"

He'd just been on the phone, taking care of that little detail. The client was hooked on the campaign he'd pitched so there was little chance of losing him by temporarily postponing their meeting over drinks at McIntyre's.

"Not anymore," he told her. "I rescheduled."

It still wasn't making any sense to her. "But why?"

He got in behind the wheel and gestured for her to get in on the passenger side. "Let's just say I'm a sucker for a damsel in distress," he told her. "Now, are you going to get in, or are we just going to stand here and talk until the store closes?" he wanted to know.

"I'm getting in," she answered, quickly doing just that. But he didn't immediately take off the way she'd expected him to. Instead, Jared paused a moment longer to input the address of the auto parts store into his GPS. Offhand, since this part of town wasn't his usual haunt, he had no idea where the store was in relation to the studio.

Replacing the GPS into its stand on the dashboard, Jared started up his car.

Elizabeth held her tongue as long as she was able, which amounted to thirty seconds before it got the better of her. "You don't know where the store is?" she asked him as they pulled out of the lot.

"No, I don't," he admitted. "But the GPS does," he assured her, flashing a wide, bright smile at her.

She found the smile stirring, and his willingness to admit that he didn't instinctively know how to find any place on the map more than admirable.

"Most men won't ask for directions," she pointed out, thinking of her father and brothers. Her brothers would rather go to their graves than admit to ignorance when it came to road travel. Her father, on the other hand, seemed to know where *everything* was and how to get there, so he had no need to ask. "They feel it somehow belittles their manhood."

"Technically, I didn't *ask* for directions," he pointed out. "I just told Gloria to find the best way to get to The Auto Mall."

"Gloria?" she echoed. Was that the name of some administrative assistant back in his office? Or did the name belong to a girlfriend?

And why would any of that even matter to her? Elizabeth silently demanded. Jared was a client—a *poten-*

tial client, she corrected herself. What he wasn't was a potential hunk.

Well; actually, she corrected herself again, he was. But the point was that he wasn't *her* potential hunk.

After all, what would she do with one of *those?* These days, what with her patchwork quilt of different gigs, she was having trouble finding the time to schedule an oil change for her car, much less anything else. When in heaven's name would she possibly find the time for a man in her life?

"That's what I call the GPS," he told her wryly. "Mine has this female voice that sounds pretty peeved with me every time I opt to ignore one of her directions. I had a teacher like that in elementary school. Her name was Mrs. Reynolds. Mrs. *Gloria* Reynolds," he emphasized. "She taught fourth grade, and it felt like nothing I ever did was right in her eyes. Every time I hear my GPS mutter 'recalculating,' I think of Mrs. Reynolds… so I just decided to call the GPS Gloria," Jared told her.

She honestly didn't know if Jared was being serious, or just pulling her leg. But whether he was or wasn't, that didn't change the fact that he was putting himself out for her.

She was grateful to him.

Manny Ramirez was just about to lock up the store for the night when a couple rushed his way.

"You the guy who called about a battery for his T-Bird?" he called out as they approached.

"It's her Thunderbird," Jared corrected, "but yeah, I'm the one who called."

"Got it right over here," the manager told them, beckoning them over to the last cash register. The battery was out of sight, stored beneath the counter. "Must be your lucky day," he told Jared. Making his way around the counter, he hefted the battery and placed it on the counter beside the register.

"Because I caught you before you closed up?" Jared asked.

The man shook his head. "Because you got the last battery I had that'll fit into the space under the hood. That's not exactly a common model," Manny told them as he rang up the sale. "Didn't get too many requests for it so I stopped carrying them." He patted the battery. "This was the last of its kind in the store. I'm not even sure if the other auto shops have it. It's usually a special-order item."

"Then I guess we really are lucky," Jared agreed, glancing at Elizabeth.

She already had her credit card out and handed it over to the manager. "We really appreciate you staying open for us."

"Hey, anytime. Nothing waiting for me at home but a wife who starts complaining the minute I walk through the door," he told them with a sigh. Taking the credit card, Manny glanced at the back to make sure it was signed. Satisfied, he swiped the magnetic strip through the card reader next to the register.

Elizabeth waited until it asked for her signature, then did the best she could to make it look legible, not an easy feat with something that resembled an Etch A Sketch.

Manny gave it a second. When he saw the words *transaction accepted,* he nodded with a smile. "Looks like you're good to go," he told them. The whole trans-action had taken under ten minutes to complete. The store manager waved them off, saying, "You two have yourselves a nice night, now."

The way he said it, Elizabeth was certain that the store manager thought they were a couple. She knew she should have corrected the man, but for a moment, she just allowed herself to enjoy the sensation of being thought of as one half of a duo. In truth, the notion of having someone standing beside her through thick and thin was incredibly tantalizing.

What surprised her most of all, though, was that Jared didn't say anything, didn't try to set the man straight.

Maybe, she mused, along with being a knight in shining armor, he was also a sensitive man who didn't like making people feel foolish or uncomfortable by pointing out their mistakes.

"Thanks, things are looking up…now that we've got this," Jared called back, indicating the battery he was carrying out of the store.

They were back in the parking lot within half an hour of initially leaving it. The guard posted at the stu-dio entrance stopped them from going in. "Need to see your ID," he said.

"But we were just here," Jared protested, taking out his driver's license. "You checked my ID before."

"And you were on the list as a visitor for the *More than Roommates* taping. But they're gone for the day and that means you should be, too." His eyes swept over both of them. It was apparent that he recognized her as well, but the same limitations applied to her as to the man he'd just denied access to the studio.

"We're not going to the soundstage," Elizabeth told the guard. "Just the parking lot."

"Lots of other parking lots to go to that aren't behind closed gates," the guard informed them.

"You don't understand. My car battery died and this man was nice enough to take me to the last auto parts store that was still open to get a new battery. It's right in the back if you don't believe me. You can come see for yourself," she urged.

"I believe you. If you were going to make up a story, it would have been more interesting than that," he groused. Pausing for a moment, as if wrestling with his conscience, he finally stepped aside. "It's against regulations, but okay, go on in. But just be quick about it," he urged.

"Absolutely. I have no intentions of spending the night here," she told the guard, then turned to look at Jared. "Thanks to you," she added.

Jared shrugged off her thanks as he drove back onto the lot and toward her vehicle. "Just trying to earn my merit badge," he cracked.

"You earned it when you found the parts guy," she responded.

"Then maybe I'll go for two," he said, pressing down on the accelerator. With most of the soundstages closed for the evening, there was far less foot and vehicle traffic and no reason to go slow.

Reaching her car, he took a flashlight out of his glove compartment and got out. Elizabeth jumped out on her side, eager to get this over with. She'd detained Jared long enough already.

He turned on the flashlight, and handed it to Elizabeth. "Here, hold this," he instructed, then gestured for her to aim the light at the inside of the open hood.

Jared took the new battery out of his backseat and brought it over to her car, setting it down on the ground. He took a long look at the defunct battery inside her car. Getting it out would have been a very simple matter—if he had the proper tools.

Staring at the dead battery now, he muttered under his breath, "Houston, we have a problem."

Elizabeth moved so that she was right next to him. Since he was staring at the battery, she looked down at it, too. "What's wrong?"

"I need tools to get the battery uncoupled and out," he told her. "Tools I don't have and forgot to pick up when we went to get the battery."

"Tools?" She moved back to her trunk. "You mean like these?" she asked, pulling a small tool box out of her trunk.

Bringing the box over to Jared, she popped open the lid and displayed a variety of tools intended just for the inner workings of a car.

"Exactly like these," he said, impressed. Those were not exactly considered to be standard accessories for a woman. "Why do you have tools like that in your trunk?"

"My dad insisted I carry these at all times, along with my jumper cables. I've had trouble with my car before, and he thought all this might come in handy someday." She grinned. "I guess this qualifies as 'someday.'" She handed the tool box over to Jared. "My dad said that I was better off driving around with them and never having to use a single one than not having them and suddenly finding myself in a real bind."

Jared heartily agreed with that philosophy. "Smart man, your father."

Nothing made her happier than hearing someone praise her dad. To her way of thinking, her father didn't get nearly as much praise as he deserved.

"That's what he's always telling me," she answered with a laugh.

Then, as she watched, Jared took off his jacket and rolled up his sleeves, displaying some very admirable forearms in the process.

Forearms that strained appealingly as he finally lifted the old battery out and set it on the ground beside the one she had just purchased.

As she continued to watch him with deliberately hooded eyes, Elizabeth began to think that maybe her battery picking this particular time to die wasn't really such a bad thing after all.

Chapter Five

The entire procedure of exchanging one battery for another and then hooking it up seemed to take a remarkably short amount of time. In Elizabeth's estimation, the trip to the shop to purchase the new battery had taken longer than the actual removal of the old battery and the installation of the new one.

When Jared announced he was "done," Elizabeth could only stare at him.

"Go ahead, try it," he urged, waving her back behind the wheel of her vehicle.

Skeptical, Elizabeth got in and turned the key in the ignition. The smooth, soothing sound of her engine coming to life and obligingly turning over was absolutely wonderful.

"You did it," she cried in relief. Up until now, she had been more or less certain that she was going to have to call a towing service.

With a nod, Jared triumphantly declared, "And we have lift off," as he wiped the smudges of oil and dirt from his hands.

"I don't know how to thank you," she exalted, leaving her engine running—just in case. It was, without a doubt, a truly beautiful sound.

Belatedly, Jared realized that the handkerchief he'd pulled out of his pocket—part of a set his mother had gifted him with, saying a gentleman never knew when he might just need a handkerchief—was probably ruined. The oil looked pretty permanent to him.

"Just play as well for my parents at their party as you did today in the studio, and that'll be thanks enough," he replied.

Elizabeth waved his suggestion away. The two weren't even in the same realm.

"That was already a given before you rode to my rescue." And then she looked down at the front of his shirt. Because of the darkness, she hadn't noticed it before. She did now. There were several streaks of what appeared to be grease on it. "Well, for starters," she told him, "I can have your shirt cleaned for you, or pay for your cleaning bill if you have a favorite cleaners you use."

He looked down at his shirt, spotting the dark streaks across the front. He didn't even remember leaning either of the batteries against himself, but obviously he must have. Grease like that didn't just leap through the air, playing a perverse game of "tag, you're it."

"Don't worry about it," he reassured her. His parents had instilled in him the edict of never throwing away money needlessly on things he could do for himself.

That included taking dress shirts to a local cleaners rather than making use of a washing machine. "I'll just throw it into the wash the way I always do."

She frowned, taking a closer look at the stains. "I don't think that's advisable," she cautioned. "The grease might spread to your other clothes and if the water happens to be hot, that stain is going to set forever." When he looked at her quizzically, she told him, "Trust me, I speak from experience. Please, let me take care of it for you."

She looked as if she wasn't going to be satisfied until he agreed. Inclining his head, he decided that saying yes to her was a lot easier than continuing this debate.

"All right, you win," he conceded.

"So you'll let me get your shirt cleaned for you?" she asked, carefully watching his expression. Instincts had taught her when she was just being humored and put off.

"Absolutely," he told her. She thought she saw the corners of his mouth curving just the slightest bit. She was right. He *was* humoring her.

"When?" she pressed.

Jared looked at her, a little surprised that she hadn't backed off since he appeared to be agreeing with her. Then, grinning, he decided to turn the tables and surprise her.

He tugged the ends of his shirt out of his waistband and started to swiftly work the buttons loose. "Well, right now if you want…" Jared murmured innocently.

Before her stunned eyes, he went down the row of buttons and from all appearances, any second now, he was literally going to give her the shirt off his back.

The next moment, surprise was trumped by appreciation as she caught more than a quick glimpse of a physique that brought the word *sculpted* to mind in glowing capital letters. This potential new client, who had so nobly come to her rescue, had very clearly defined pectorals and looked as if he spent every waking spare moment in the gym.

Elizabeth could feel all the moisture evaporate from her mouth even as she searched for something intelligent to say—or at least not stutter like some dazed teenager when she spoke.

She finally found her tongue, which felt as if it had been stuck to the roof of her mouth. "I didn't mean that you had to give me your shirt this very second."

"Oh, sorry," he apologized impishly. "I misunderstood."

He hadn't.

What he'd decided to do was see just how far Elizabeth was going to push this need she seemed to have for instant payback. Very slowly, he began to rebutton his shirt.

There was humor in his eyes as he said, "Then it's all right with you if I give the shirt to you, say, the next time we get together?"

"Absolutely," she answered with more than a little enthusiasm and relief.

Her relief was short-lived as something else suddenly dawned on her. Jared was buttoning up his shirt and covering up again, so why did she still feel as if she was physically standing on top of a burning bush? It certainly hadn't been this hot in the parking lot a few minutes ago. Just where had this blast of heat come from?

Blowing out a breath, she found her voice, although she had to admit that it sounded a touch shaky to her ear. Especially when she went on to say more than just a single word.

"I know of another way to repay you."

He looked at her, one eyebrow raised sardonically as a scenario he *knew* she'd had no intention of acting on suggested itself to him.

"Oh?" he asked, doing his best to make the word sound a great deal more innocent than his thoughts currently were at this moment.

Judging by the hue that had suddenly begun to creep up her cheeks, he realized that he wasn't being altogether successful in keeping a lid on it. Apparently, he had somehow managed to at least partially telegraph his less-than-chaste vision to her.

"Dinner," she all but choked out. "If you postponed your meeting until another day, I was going to suggest dinner." It was all that she could do to keep from stumbling over the simple words.

Dinner definitely had some appeal, he thought. Actually, the idea of an intimate setting with the woman was what actually held the most appeal for him.

Intrigued, Jared asked, "You mean a home-cooked meal?"

That quickly snapped her out of the very warm place she'd found herself slipping into.

Elizabeth laughed as she shook her head. "Oh God, no. I want to thank you, not kill you or send you to the intensive care unit of the nearest hospital. What kind of way would that be to pay you back and say thank you?" she wanted to know.

Her laugh melded with his as he tucked the edge of his shirt back underneath his waistband. "Your cooking can't be all that bad."

Spoken like a man who'd never sampled her cooking efforts, she mused. Elizabeth knew what she could do and knew her limitations as well. Cooking definitely came under the heading of the latter.

"I wouldn't take any bets if I were you," she advised. "Not unless you really like losing. Even my father, who thinks the sun rises and sets around me, will tell you that if you value your life, don't eat anything I've had a hand in preparing."

"He thinks the sun rises and sets around you, huh?" Jared repeated, intrigued as well as amused. "Let me guess, you're the only girl in the family."

"I'm impressed. You got it on the first try. Yes, I'm the only girl."

He tightened the parameters a little more and asked, "Only child?"

She shook her head. "Nope. I have two younger brothers. So much for your winning streak. You're slipping."

He took her taunting in stride. "Just didn't want you to get the wrong idea and feel as if you were in the presence of a clairvoyant."

Her amusement reached her eyes, managing to capture him the moment he noticed it. "Is that what you think you are, a clairvoyant?"

He could tell by the way she asked that she didn't believe in people who claimed to see into the future.

That made two of them. But he decided to tease her a little longer. "Let's just say I have exceptionally good instincts when it comes to making decent calculated guesses about people. So, since your father dotes on you, does your mother dote on your brothers, or does one of them feel as if he's getting shortchanged?"

The moment he asked about her mother, she could feel the wave of sadness sweep over her. Wasn't that ever going to stop?

"I think we all got kind of shortchanged, actually." When the quizzical look on his face deepened, she offered him a sliver of the story she rarely shared with anyone.

"My mother died when I was five. My brothers were still babies when she left our lives." There was an incredible amount of sadness in her voice.

Jared felt instantly guilty for having brought up something that obviously hurt her so much. "I'm really sorry, I didn't mean to dredge up any painful memories for you."

"You didn't," she assured him, and she was being truthful. "Any memories I have of her are cherished, not buried because it hurts too much to remember her. Memories—and her violin—are all I have of her," she explained.

"Now, about that dinner," Elizabeth began, deftly switching topics. She was rather convinced that Jared was pretty vulnerable to a blitzkrieg right now, seeing as how he obviously thought he'd upset her with his unintentional comment. "I haven't had anything to eat since before lunch, and because I've imposed on you to help me, I know for a fact that you haven't had dinner yet. So why don't I show you my gratitude by buying you dinner at the restaurant of your choice? The sky's

the limit," she told him. "As long as the sky's relatively
low," she qualified with a grin that he found infinitely
appealing.

"We could pick up a package of hot dogs and hold
them over a fire," he suggested, doing his best to keep
a straight face. As far as he was concerned, she didn't
owe him anything. He liked being helpful.

Elizabeth shook her head. "I told you, I can't cook,"
she pointed out.

"That's not cooking, that's holding a stick over a fire
and occasionally moving your wrist back and forth,"
he protested.

She greeted his explanation with, "Potato, po-tot-to.
That's still considered cooking in some circles—and
grilling in others." She had a feeling that Jared thought
she was kidding about her culinary abilities—or in-
abilities as the case was. She wasn't. "For everyone's
well-being all around, I'd *really* rather have a professional take care of preparing the meal."

Jared laughed, surrendering. "Okay, you win. No
cooking. All right, why don't *you* pick the restaurant,"
he told her.

That wasn't good enough. "I'm thanking you, it's
only fair that you pick," she told him, remaining firm.

She came on soft and sweet, but he was beginning to
wonder if *anyone* ever won an argument with this woman.
"All right," he surrendered, "How about Giuseppe's?"

She was familiar with the establishment. "Pizza?"
she asked.

The restaurant he'd picked was known for its Ital-
ian cuisine in general, but its real specialty was pizza.

All sorts of pizza. Thick or thin or stuffed, it offered an almost endless variety of toppings.

Jared nodded. "I love pizza," he told her earnestly.

She was still rather skeptical about his choice—she knew the restaurant wasn't expensive and had a hunch that was what was really responsible for his choice. He didn't want her spending a lot of money. His gallantry reminded her of something that her father would have done.

"Really?" she asked, deliberately scrutinizing his expression.

"Really," he told her, never wavering. For good measure, he crossed his heart.

Elizabeth gave in. Maybe he was on the level. "Okay. Giuseppe's it is," she agreed. "I'll meet you there," she told him.

"Fair enough." He got into his vehicle and leaned out to say something further.

But it was too late. She was already starting up her car.

They did start out at the same time, since their vehicles were parked next to each other. But five minutes into the journey, after stopping at a light that was about to turn red in less than the next heartbeat, Jared discovered that he'd lost her.

Elizabeth hadn't stopped. Instead, she'd flown through the light and actually made it to the other side of the intersection before the light finished turning red.

Close to half an hour later, Jared finally pulled up into the popular eatery's parking lot. The traffic there had been lighter than normal, but it had still come under the heading of "traffic," which, in California-speak, meant bumper-to-bumper for at least part of the distance.

Halfway to the restaurant, he'd opted to take an overland route rather than continue traveling on the freeway, which was misnamed if anything ever had been, he thought darkly.

Parking his vehicle at the edge of the crowded lot, Jared made his way toward the short, squat building, heading for the restaurant's entrance. He fully expected to have to stand around in front of the double doors, waiting for Elizabeth to arrive. Though he'd kept a vigilant eye out for her, he hadn't seen any sign of the woman's vintage vehicle as he drove to the restaurant.

He was spared the wait...because Elizabeth was already there.

And, from her cool and calm appearance, she'd been standing there by the entrance awhile now.

It took him a bit of effort to keep the stunned expression off his face.

She smiled warmly at him when she saw him approaching the front door. "Hi."

"Hi," he echoed. "You didn't tell me that your car was refitted with wings and doubled as a hovercraft."

She caught the slightly sarcastic tone. Had she tread on his male ego by unintentionally beating him in a time-honored male sport, auto racing?

"It wasn't and doesn't." She pulled the door open and was a little taken aback when she saw his arm go out just above her head and take possession of the door away from her. She could almost *see* his biceps flexing as he effortlessly held the heavy, double-wide door open for her.

"I have what my family likes to refer to as a lead foot," she explained, then confessed, "It's not something I'm overly proud of. I really do try to rein it in, but there's something about making a light just before it turns red and squeaking through tight places that I find to be really irresistible—no matter how hard I try to ignore it, or at least not give in to the temptation. Just between you and me, I *really* have trouble resisting the allure of going fast."

"Remind me never to have you drive me anywhere," he quipped.

"Unless it's an emergency," she pointed out. "Then you might be happy I can make twists and turns most people turn pale just thinking about."

He took her at her word about the pale part. "Just how many traffic tickets have you amassed?" he asked, curious.

"None, actually." She could see he was going to need convincing. "I don't run red lights and I don't go above posted speed limits."

"The key word here being *posted*," he guessed wryly.

When she merely smiled at him in response to his comment, her eyes dancing, he had his answer. Why he found her to be so appealing when she made her admission, he wasn't really able to say. He was accustomed to women who worried about the wind messing with their hair, or not being the sole object of interest when they entered a room.

Elizabeth, apparently, had no concerns about turning heads, or literally having every hair in place. She appeared to be far too full of life to be overly worried about things like that.

He supposed that was her Bohemian spirit, coming to the forefront. He found he rather liked it.

Liked it? he silently mocked himself. Hell, he found it downright captivating.

"Two?" the hostess asked, coming up to greet them the moment they stepped into the restaurant.

"Two," he confirmed.

He caught himself thinking that there was something oddly comfortable about being part of a duo, even if only for the length of time that it took to eat a meal. Most of the time, when he went out to eat and he wasn't using that time to court a company client, he was alone. For the most part, his meals were sporadic, spur-of-the-moment decisions and thus, perforce, very solitary affairs.

The idea of sharing a meal with someone without having to pitch ideas and be ever vigilant and on his toes was exceedingly appealing to him.

Jared caught himself smiling as he followed the hostess and Elizabeth into the heart of the restaurant. He was going to enjoy this, he promised himself.

He had a hunch that he was going to enjoy sitting opposite Elizabeth as he ate even more.

Chapter Six

"Have you been doing this long?" he asked Elizabeth once the hostess had given them their menus and quietly retreated from their table.

The question had caught her completely off guard. For a second, she wasn't sure what he was referring to. "You mean eating? For as long as I can remember."

Jared laughed. He'd found that a sense of humor was an indispensable tool when it came to being able not just to survive, but to survive well. He liked hers. If he were ever in the market for a wife—which of course he wasn't—a sense of humor would have been his number one priority.

Having legs that didn't quit and a face that daydreams were made of didn't exactly detract from the total picture, either.

But he wasn't looking for a mate, nor would he ever be. He didn't like failing, and most marriages today never saw the light of their fifth anniversary, much less their thirty-fifth. His parents had a marriage that was damn near close to perfect. If he couldn't have that—and odds in today's world were pretty great that he couldn't—he didn't want any marriage at all.

"That part I just assumed," he told Elizabeth. "I meant playing. As in how long have you been playing the violin?"

"Almost as long as I've been eating," Elizabeth answered.

She saw the slight dubious look that came into Jared's eyes. She didn't want him thinking that she was telling him she'd been a child prodigy, because she wasn't. She'd just been a little girl who was trying to make contact with a mother who was gone.

"I feel like it's in my blood," she explained. "My parents met at a concert during college. She was playing, he was listening." Those were her mother's exact words, she recalled fondly. "Dad told me that the first time he heard her play, he felt as if he were in the presence of an angel."

Jared saw a sad expression play across her face as she went on talking.

"When my mother died, he told me that God wanted to have nothing but beautiful music around Him, so He took her to heaven." She looked at Jared and wondered if he thought she was being rather simple-minded. "When you're five, you believe everything your father tells you." A rueful smile curved her lips. "I was really angry at God for about a year."

"At that age, I would have been, too," Jared agreed gently.

He was humoring her, she thought, but it was still rather nice of him. She flashed him a quick, grateful smile.

"Anyway, holding her violin made me feel closer to her, as if a part of her were still there somehow, so I asked my father if I could have lessons. He made the arrangements, even got me the same instructor who initially taught my mother," she confided. "The woman couldn't get over how much I looked like my mother. By the end of the year, Ms. Jablonsky said I played the violin just like my mother, too.

"I don't think I ever received a better compliment—unless it was seeing the tears in my dad's eyes when I played in my very first recital. He said it was like being at that concert when he met my mother all over again. He told me that my mother would have been proud of me."

Elizabeth realized that, just for a moment, she'd let her guard down and gotten misty. Clearing her throat, she pushed back the feelings that were welling up inside her, and blinked her eyes, determined to keep her tears from falling.

"Anyway, I found that I loved playing, just for its own sake," she concluded.

The pizza arrived and the discussion was temporarily tabled as they both made small talk, commenting on how good the pizza smelled, etc. Jared confessed that he hadn't realized just how hungry he actually was until the aroma had hit him.

"I tend to forget to eat when I get busy or distracted," he confided.

Did she come under the heading of being a distraction? Elizabeth wondered. Or was he saying that he'd considered coming to hear her play on the soundstage as "being busy"?

She realized that, given a choice, she would have preferred having the good-looking man think of her as a distraction. The implications of that were far more promising.

You're letting your imagination get the better of you. That's what you get for listening to Amanda.

Amanda was one of the other violinists. They'd initially met in high school, had wound up going to the same college and had gradually become best friends. Amanda was the one who kept telling her that she needed to get "really emotionally, soulfully involved" with someone in order to bring a deeper meaning to her music. Her friend's theory was that until she experienced falling in love, and then losing that love, she couldn't truly make her violin weep.

Her answer to Amanda was that she was willing to settle on having her violin sob quietly. What she didn't admit to her close confidante was that she'd gone the romance route and been rather badly disappointed. That was no one's business but her own.

"I don't think I've *ever* forgotten to eat," she told Jared. "My stomach is very good about reminding me that it needs to be periodically fed."

So saying, she liberated a piece from the rest of the pizza and, rather than put it on her plate, she brought the pointed edge up to her lips and proceeded to take a good-size bite.

Her eyes fluttered shut as she allowed herself to

slowly savor the taste. "This is really good," she enthused.

Watching her, just for a moment, Jared found himself caught up in the way she was relishing her food. Most of the women he'd gone out with seemed to pick at their meal, eating little and appearing to enjoy it even less. Eating pizza, especially the way Elizabeth did, would have been viewed as something that was beneath them. Eating with their hands was simply not done. "Uncivilized barbarians ate with their hands" was the way one of his dates had put it.

He smiled to himself now, watching Elizabeth. There was definitely something to be said for "uncivilized barbarians," he thought.

"I know," he agreed. "That's why I suggested coming here. I'd rather have a good pizza than practically anything else. I think I actually horrified my sister by casually suggesting we have pizza at my parents' anniversary celebration. I had to reassure her that I was kidding."

Elizabeth scrutinized his handsome face for a moment. "But you weren't kidding, were you?" she surmised. Before he could answer, she asked, "Do your parents like pizza?"

"They do," he admitted. "But I have a feeling that some of their friends will ask them if I've suddenly fallen on hard times if I have their thirty-fifth anniversary catered with pizza."

Personally, she liked that idea. Serving something simple that most people really enjoyed. She firmly believed in the "life is short" adage and felt that people should be able to do what they liked—as long as it didn't hurt anyone else—and having pizza certainly wasn't hurting anyone.

Subtly, she tried to steer Jared toward rethinking his menu choice. "You know, there're a lot of different varieties of pizza—you could go all out and have the caterer come up with, oh, twelve or so different kinds so that people could have their choice and still have pizza. Frankly, in my opinion, having all those different kinds to choose from beats having to eat a single, set meal."

Maybe she had something there, Jared thought, turning the idea over in his head.

"It does, doesn't it?" he said thoughtfully. "Still, I know how my sister'd react, and, frankly, there isn't a meal in the world that's worth having to endure Megan's ire when she goes on a tirade." He shrugged. "Going along with her choices saves a lot of wear and tear on a person's nerves. And lately, she's been more high-strung than usual, but then that's to be expected, I guess."

He realized by the silent, befuddled look on Elizabeth's face that he'd left out a single, rather salient detail in his narrative.

"Oh, I think I forgot to mention that my sister's pregnant with her first child. And right now, not the most patient of people—not that she was exactly the soul of patience before."

In all honesty, they couldn't *wait* until the ordeal was finally over—and she still had three months to go. Just before his sister left on a cruise that her husband had booked for them as a surprise, Megan had been lamenting that she already felt so huge. Jared had tried to persuade her otherwise on numerous occasions…

but there was no consoling her when she called him in hysterics from the cruise ship terminal because a fellow passenger asked if she was carrying twins! He still shuddered every time he remembered that excruciatingly awkward phone call.

"Yes, you forgot to mention your sister's condition," Elizabeth responded with a nod. "That does explain why you're tiptoeing around her." Although she really only had his word that that was what he was doing, she added silently.

She was well aware that brothers had a definite tendency to exaggerate details when it came to their sisters. However, Jared did come across as very genuine in his concern for his sister. Elizabeth smiled at him. The man did seem to have hidden qualities that she found quite admirable and appealing.

"You know," she told him, "for a brother, you're awfully sensitive and thoughtful."

"For a brother?" he echoed, somewhat bemused. "Care to explain that?"

Elizabeth nodded, holding up her finger to silently indicate that he was going to have to wait a second longer for her to elaborate. First, she needed to swallow what she'd just bitten off.

"I have two brothers," she told him the second she could, "and I know for a fact that they would relish irritating me about absolutely anything rather than being mindful of my feelings. Hence, since you're being so considerate of your sister's condition, that would make you sensitive and thoughtful."

He couldn't see anyone actually deliberately trying to get under her skin. Under her clothes, maybe, but—

Almost startled by the direction his mind had just wandered off in, he abruptly shut down his thoughts. He needed to exercise a little better self-control than he'd been doing. For heaven's sake, he was planning music for his parents' anniversary celebration, not for a quick tryst of his own.

Clearing his throat, he focused on what she'd just told him and not on the image that had popped up in his head. "They're probably just good at hiding their true feelings about you."

She laughed shortly. "No, my brothers aren't trying to hide anything," she guaranteed. "I'm very aware of how they feel about me. I'm their big sister, the one they always went to to borrow money from or to run interference for them with our dad whenever they did something stupid. The one who always wound up lecturing them about it."

"And did you?" When she looked at him in confusion, he framed his question more succinctly. "Lend them money and run interference?"

Elizabeth shrugged, avoiding making eye contact and looking at the remainder of the pizza on the tray rather than at him.

"I'd like to say no, I didn't, but I really seem to have trouble saying that word when it comes to family," she divulged. And then she rethought her words. Her confession wasn't broad enough, she decided. "Actually, I have trouble saying no to anyone."

The moment she made the statement, she realized how that had to sound to him. As if she was some pushover people easily had their way with. She definitely didn't want him getting that impression. "I mean, as in doing someone a favor, not as in anything that…"

She was searching for a graceful way out of this, he realized. Jared had no desire to see her twisting in the wind like this. "I understand what you mean," he assured her.

She breathed a quick sigh of relief, not altogether sure just how she'd managed to paint herself into that kind of a corner. She didn't ordinarily get flustered or tongue-tied. And she was usually a great deal clearer when she spoke.

Had to be those mesmerizing green eyes of his, she concluded. Every time she gazed into them, they seemed to completely undermine her ability to think coherently.

His eyes seemed to have the exact same effect on her pulse rate. It hadn't really settled down since she'd spotted him standing off to the side, listening to her play on the soundstage.

"New topic," she declared, feeling it was the only way to start over. She returned to what she knew: music. It was the only safe topic available to her. "Are you going to want to have an ensemble playing at your parents' party, a band, or what?"

Amused at her choice of wording, he asked, "What's an 'or what'?"

Elizabeth didn't even hesitate. "Anything you want it to be," she informed him.

The word *want* seemed to pulse in his mind for a split second. What he found himself wanting at that moment had nothing to do with orchestrated music and everything to do with the woman sitting opposite him in the small booth.

After a beat, he realized that while the eatery was far from silent, the silence between them was drawing out. She was obviously waiting for an answer and expected him to make a decision right here and now. Not that waiting would be of any help.

He went with his gut.

"A band, I guess," he responded.

"What sort of musicians do you want in this band?" Elizabeth pressed, wanting to get as much information out of him as possible. She didn't want him to think that she was going to manipulate him into giving her friends jobs as well.

Jared shrugged. He definitely hadn't thought this part out—or had even been aware of it. When Mrs. Manetti had suggested music for the party and given him Elizabeth's name, it had seemed like a good idea. It had also seemed like a complete idea, not one that required more decisions.

"Good ones," he finally told her.

She pressed her lips together to keep the laugh that had risen back. "Besides that."

He thought for a moment, trying to recall something he'd once seen. "Someone to play the keyboard, maybe a guitar…"

He was searching, she realized. The next question she asked him was for form's sake, already rather certain she knew his answer. "Have you hired anyone else for this band?"

"No," he answered, then confided, "I'm really kind of new at this."

For the second time, humor tugged at her mouth, a laugh bubbling up in her throat. She suppressed it. Men didn't appreciate being laughed at, no matter how much they deserved to be.

"You could have fooled me," she said with as straight a face as she could manage, under the circumstances.

He saw right through her. "No, I couldn't," Jared said.

Elizabeth released the laugh that all but begged to be freed.

"Okay, you couldn't," she allowed, quickly following that with a distracting, practical suggestion. "Why don't we discuss the kind of music your parents would enjoy hearing at their party and, in addition, what you might want to hear played. If you tell me that, I can try to figure out the kind of instruments you're going to need for this 'band.'" He looked to be a little stumped by her suggestion, so she tried to simplify it for him as much as possible. "To begin with, how many people do you envision playing in this 'band'?"

In his mind's eye, he'd seen a handful. "Five sound like a good number to you?" he asked her. "You're the expert, after all."

Now there he was wrong. She played violin, she didn't put together bands or ensembles. At least, not until now. "I'm not an expert," she protested.

He wasn't about to retreat from his assessment. "Compared to me, you are."

Elizabeth inclined her head, conceding for now.

"Point taken. Yes, five's a good number," she allowed. She took a breath. Depending on the kind of songs he wanted played, the instrument she played might not even be the best for what he had in mind. "At the risk of talking myself out of a job, are you sure you really want a violin in this mix?"

He looked at her, his eyes instantly taking hers prisoner. Elizabeth was certain she felt something electrifying zigzagging through her body at just under the speed of light.

"Absolutely," he told her.

There went her pulse again, she thought. *Focus, Liz, focus,* she silently ordered.

"All right," she said out loud. "The keyboard's a good suggestion and you might want to think about getting a cellist as well. That way, you could run the gamut of music from classical, to jazz to pop." She watched him, chewing on her bottom lip as she waited to see what he thought of her suggestion.

From out of nowhere, a jolt of desire ambushed him. He would have blamed the whole thing on the wine— except that he hadn't had any tonight. Rousing himself, he realized that she was waiting for a response from him.

It took him a moment to recall what she'd just said. Or at least part of it. "Sounds good to me."

"All right, I know a cellist who's reasonable—and good," she emphasized in case he thought she was just trying to get work for a friend. "And there's this musician I know who can practically get a keyboard to talk—" She paused for a second, deciding she needed a little more input from him. "You know, it would really help if you could give me the names of a few of the songs your parents like to listen to."

He would if he could, but for the life of him, not a

single song title came to mind. His mind still a blank after several attempts, he finally said, "That would be my sister's department."

Fair enough. She doubted if either one of her brothers knew the title of a single song their father liked. "When do you think I could meet her?" she asked.

That was going to be tricky, he thought. "Megan's not around right now. Her husband booked this cruise as a surprise for her way before they knew she was pregnant and the deposit was nonrefundable—so they went," he told her. "Megan didn't want to hurt his feelings—this is the first thing Max, her husband, ever planned on his own, and she's afraid that if she squelched it, he'd give up and never try to surprise her again. But I have to admit that this is really cutting things rather close. She's coming back two days before the party."

And that wound up putting the burden of keeping track of all the arrangements for this celebration squarely on his shoulders.

"Okay, we'll approach this from another angle," Elizabeth said gamely. "Do your parents have a CD collection?"

She saw him smile at that. "Vinyl," he told her. "They have an old vinyl collection."

Things clicked in her head. Even better. "They like the oldies," she concluded.

This was promising…

A light came into his green eyes, making them even more magnetic, in her opinion, than they already were. "Yeah, I guess they do."

"Great. Now we're getting somewhere." Wiping her

fingers off on a napkin, Elizabeth dug into her purse and pulled out a pen and pad, ready to jot everything down. "Do they have a favorite artist, group or style?" And then she held up her hand to stop him in case he was going to tell her that he didn't know. "When you were a kid, do you remember the music they played? Close your eyes," she prompted.

"Why?"

"It helps. Trust me."

He shrugged. "Okay." And he shut his eyes.

"Now, what do you hear? Concentrate," she underscored.

He took a deep breath and did as she suggested. His mind drifted back over the years. For a long moment, he was very quiet. And then he heard it, heard a fragment of a melody transcending time.

"I think my dad liked listening to the Rolling Stones," he said. Yes, it was definitely the Stones, he thought, a note of triumph echoing through his veins. "My mother tended to favor something Dad referred to as 'bubblegum music.' He'd tease her about it. She'd turn up the volume to drown him out." His eyes flew open and he looked at Elizabeth, somewhat stunned. "I'd forgotten all about that," he confessed, a note of pleasure in his voice.

Elizabeth nodded, her smile all but radiant. "This is good," she told him. "Very good. I can bring over a sample of some of the old CDs my father has so we can home in on some of your folks' favorite songs. We'll get a playlist together that they'll love—and your sister will approve of," she added for good measure.

Jared leaned back in his seat and watched as Elizabeth got rolling and picked up steam.

As he listened to this vibrant dynamo pull things together, he silently blessed Theresa Manetti for bringing Elizabeth Stephens into his life.

For possibly more than one reason.

Chapter Seven

"Are you sure you're not forgetting something?" Megan Winterset MacDonald pressed, her usual friendly tone bordering perilously close to impatience after her brother had assured her that everything was "fine."

Even on this ship-to-shore call, Jared could vividly envision the furrows forming on his sister's brow. "No, I'm not forgetting something, Megan. You left me a list, remember?"

"And you didn't lose it?" she wanted to know, sounding skeptical.

"If you recall, you anchored it with four magnets onto my refrigerator and, so far, I'm happy to report that I haven't lost my refrigerator." He loved Megan dearly and they'd built up a good relationship once they'd left their teens, but there were times when he could totally recall why he had once dubbed her Princess Royal Pain.

"Correct me if I'm wrong, but aren't you supposed to be having fun right now?" he reminded her.

He heard her sigh—most likely the entire cruise ship heard her sigh, he thought.

"I'd be having more fun if Max had scheduled this cruise for some other time," she complained.

"Because of the baby?" Jared asked sympathetically. Being seasick and pregnant was just about the worst combination he could think of.

"No. Aren't you paying attention?" she accused. "Because of Mom and Dad's anniversary party. I don't like leaving everything on your shoulders."

"They're broad shoulders, Megan. Besides, you did insist on setting almost everything in motion before you left," he reminded her.

"Almost?" she asked suspiciously. "What do you mean, 'almost'? Jared, what did you do?"

He noticed that she didn't ask him what she had forgotten to do. Her immediate assumption was that he'd done something wrong.

Because he loved her and Megan *was* pregnant, which meant her hormones were all over the map, he let the accusation slide, and calmly explained what was currently going on.

"Mrs. Manetti asked me if we were having music at the party and I told her I hadn't thought about it. She said that she thought it would be a nice touch and gave me the name of this really talented violinist—"

Megan immediately cut in. "Jared, Mrs. Manetti's a very nice woman who doesn't have a bad word to say about anyone. You can't just take her word for it that this guy's talented—"

"It's a woman, not a man," Jared corrected, heading his sister off before she could launch into a long lecture. Megan was his junior by three years, but there were times that she behaved as if she were his older sister and he was the younger, idiot brother. He told himself that she had control issues and that, in his own way, her husband, Max, was a saint. "And I went to hear her play for myself. If anything, Mrs. Manetti was conservative in her praise."

"You went to hear this woman play? Where was she playing?" Before he could answer, she groaned as if she could predict what he was about to say. "And please don't tell me it was some bar."

Okay, she was really going overboard here. "Not that I know of…but why would that even matter?" Everyone had to start somewhere.

He heard her blow out a frustrated breath. "I didn't mean to imply there's anything wrong with someone working in a bar."

"Yes, you did, Megan," he replied tolerantly. "Just because someone might take an initial job that is beneath your standards, doesn't automatically make those people socially unacceptable."

He could have sworn he heard her voice quaver a little as she conceded. "Point taken. It's just that I want this party to be perfect. Mom and Dad are going to have only one thirty-fifth anniversary."

Thank God for small favors, he thought. Out loud he merely agreed with her. He'd found that, in the long run, it was a lot easier that way. "I know, Megan—and it'll be fine. Trust me on this."

"Trust you," she echoed, releasing a harsh laugh.

"You've never thrown a party for more than two people in your life."

"No." He saw no reason to dispute that, since he hadn't. Parties were his sister's domain, not his. And his circle of friends—real friends, not clients he was wooing—was rather small and very casual. "But I've attended a few. And," he reminded her again, "I have that list you left me to refer to if I get lost or think I've forgotten to do something crucial. Now stop worrying…it's all going to be great. And you'll be back in plenty of time to rubber-stamp everything—or override me," he added, knowing how she tended to think.

He heard his sister pausing on the other end. There were voices in the background, but whether it was because someone was talking to Megan or because it was just general background noise on the cruise ship, he couldn't tell.

"Not fast enough for me," she confided, lowering her voice. The fact that she did made him think that her husband had to be close by. He'd given her this cruise with the best of intentions, not realizing that Megan wasn't captivated by the idea of going on a cruise—and that she'd be close to six months pregnant when it came time to sail.

"Hang in there, Megan," he encouraged. "And *don't worry*," he repeated with emphasis. "I'm holding down the fort."

"I know you are, and I'm sorry," she apologized, completely surprising him. Megan *rarely* apologized. "This being pregnant has my emotions just all over the place. I didn't mean to take it out on you."

"And this is different from your normal state how?" he asked innocently.

She appreciated that he didn't get soft on her. She didn't need that right now. "Consider my apology rescinded and remind me to beat you to a pulp when I get back."

"I'll make a note, and put it on the refrigerator right next to your list," he informed her solemnly.

"You do that." She sighed. "Better go—this call is costing me a fortune. We'll talk soon," she said before hanging up.

"Not if I remember to look at caller ID first," he muttered into the silent receiver.

He did love her, but she could make him absolutely crazy with all that misplaced nervous energy she was displaying lately.

Shaking his head, he replaced the receiver into the cradle. He'd just removed his hand from it when the phone rang again.

With a sigh, he yanked it back up to his ear, bracing himself for round two. "Did you suddenly remember something else you wanted to berate me about?" he wanted to know.

There was a long, drawn-out pause on the other end of the line. And then he heard a somewhat uncertain voice say, "No, I just wanted you to know I found some other musicians I thought you might want to hear play."

Oh damn, he thought. It *wasn't* his sister calling to tell him one more thing as was her habit.

"Elizabeth?" he asked uncertainly, even though he'd recognized her voice. He'd never wanted to be so wrong in his life. Since it most likely *was* Elizabeth, the woman probably thought she was dealing with a village idiot.

"Yes," she replied, sounding every bit as uncertain as he just did.

The truth shall set you free, remember, buddy? Hence, he decided he was better off coming clean with Elizabeth. "I'm sorry, I thought you were Megan again. My sister," he explained in case he hadn't mentioned her name to Elizabeth.

She knew how irritating siblings could be at times. "I take it you two aren't getting along."

"Actually, most of the time we do," he corrected. "But when she goes off the deep end about something, she turns into this whole other, completely overbearing creature."

Elizabeth was trying to make sense out of something she'd obviously just gotten in the middle of. "And she went off the deep end?"

"Oh yeah," he answered with emphasis. "Big-time. She's really stressing out about this anniversary party that we're throwing for our parents."

Now it was beginning to make sense. "Didn't you tell me that your sister was going through her first pregnancy?"

"She's close to six months along," he confirmed.

"*And* that she's currently on a cruise with her husband?"

"Yes. Actually, the cruise was a surprise gift from her husband." He was all for surprises, but they were a lot better when it was something the recipient actually *liked*. "You'd think that after five years together, he'd know that she wasn't keen on being on a ship in the middle of the Pacific," he said as an aside.

"She doesn't *like* cruises?" Elizabeth asked incredulously.

"Not so much." Which was actually a polite understatement.

"Well, there's the reason for her going overboard," Elizabeth deduced. "That's a lot for a person to juggle all at the same time while still worrying about a big party and trying to make certain that all the details for its successful execution are in order. Any one of those things could really floor someone."

He'd listened in amusement as she took on the part of being his sister's advocate. "You always take the side of people you don't know?" he asked.

"I'm not taking sides," she informed him. "I'm just seeing the whole picture. I have a tendency to do that. Insert myself into things," she revealed. "Did you tell your sister about me?"

"About you?" he repeated, a little confused. Did she think that Megan would object to his planning things with her?

"Yes. About me," she said again. The silence on the other end told her that maybe she needed to elaborate on that before he got the wrong idea. "Did you tell her that I'll be playing at your parents' anniversary party?" The longer the silence on the other end of the phone, the tighter the knot in her stomach became. A knot that had materialized for no apparent reason…

Isn't there a reason? something whispered in her head. *Haven't you caught him looking at you in a way that made you forget all about the music you were sup-*

*posed to play and made you think about the music the
two of you could produce, given half a chance?*

Oh boy, where had that come from? she silently wondered. Granted, she'd seen him a number of times over
the past few days, mainly to go over pieces she'd selected to play, pieces she wanted to make sure that his
parents were fond of. And okay, maybe she'd drawn out
the process a little so that she could spend a bit more
time with him than was needed, but on the other hand,
he kept asking to get together, telling her that he preferred dealing with "people" one-on-one rather than
just talking to them over the phone.

If he were really flirting with her, she staunchly told
herself, he wouldn't have just lumped her together with
"people" like that. It was too broad a category. If a man
wanted a woman to feel he was paying attention to her,
he would have phrased the whole thing differently.

Wouldn't he?

She had no answer for that, mainly because she
didn't know. Her experience when it came to men outside the realm of work was limited mostly to her father
and her brothers—and the latter didn't count.

Oh, there had been a boyfriend once as well. Geoffrey. But he didn't count, either. Geoffrey just wanted
someone so that he could bask in her attention, bask in
the light in her eyes when she looked at him. The problem she eventually found out was that it didn't really
matter who "she" was. As long as she had the required
love light in her eyes and was willing to make him the
center of her universe, that was all that truly mattered
to Geoffrey.

Once she'd realized that, the two of them had parted

company, with Geoffrey snidely telling her she was going to be sorry, that she didn't realize what she was giving up and that she'd be back.

That had happened a little over four years ago. She wondered if he'd given up waiting for her to come back yet.

"Yes," Jared was saying. "I told Megan about hiring you so that there'd be live music at my parents' anniversary party. I think I really surprised my sister by undertaking something that she hadn't left on her famous list."

Elizabeth picked up on the sarcasm in Jared's voice. A tone-deaf person could have heard it. "Her 'famous' list?"

"Before she left, Megan wrote up a to-do list for me, covering all the things she wanted me to check on while she was away on the cruise." He realized that probably sounded as if he'd been slaving away, making arrangements for the party. He didn't want to take any undue credit since Megan had done the bulk of the slaving.

"Basically, the list just goes over everything she'd already set in motion herself. She wanted me to make sure that it was all getting done, all on schedule." He laughed shortly. "In essence, what she was asking me to do was to hound people."

Elizabeth focused on the pertinent part of what he'd just said. At least, it was pertinent to her. "And music wasn't on her list?"

"No, it wasn't." Which, when he thought about it now, surprised him. It was a definite omission and he was glad he'd corrected it. And *really* glad he'd taken

Mrs. Manetti's recommendation to heart. Otherwise, he would have never met Elizabeth.

Elizabeth drew her own conclusions based on the things he'd just said—and what he tactfully hadn't said. "And your sister wasn't exactly happy about your initiative."

"She likes to be in charge."

She paused for a moment, thinking. While the salary they had agreed on for that evening's performance was more than generous, and she certainly welcomed it, she really didn't like the idea of being a source of discord between Jared and his sister. If it came down to that, she knew that if she did play at his parents' party, she would wind up feeling very guilty about it.

No amount of money was worth feeling bad.

"Look," she began, coming to the only decision she could, "I understand."

"You understand?" Jared repeated, more than a little confused. "Well, maybe *you* do," he granted, "but I know that I don't. Exactly what is it that you understand?"

All right, maybe she needed to spell it out for him. "I don't like causing problems or coming between people, especially family members. I'll just tell the others that there's been a change of plans and that they won't need to individually audition for you."

"Hold it, back up," he told her. "*What* change of plans?" Nobody had said anything to that effect. Just what was she talking about anyway?

Why was he making her jump through these hoops when she was just trying to make it easy on him?

"About hiring a band and having live music at your parents' anniversary party."

"Did I miss something here?" he asked, allowing his complete confusion to come through. "We're still throwing my parents a surprise thirty-fifth anniversary party and that party still needs live music. Wait," he said as he suddenly realized that maybe he was focusing on this from the wrong end. "Are you telling me that you're backing out?"

"No!" Elizabeth denied emphatically. "I'm not backing out. I'm just trying to make this easy on you."

"Make *what* easy on me?" he wanted to know. "Just how does confusing me make things easier?"

And where the hell had she gotten that idea in the first place? He certainly hadn't mentioned anything to her, certainly nothing to give her an inkling of what Megan thought of his lone contribution to the party.

"Look, I'm pretty much an uncomplicated guy," he told her. "What you see is what you get. If I change my mind about something and that something involves you, you'll know about it."

God knew—going along with his declaration—she would have been more than happy to grab what she saw and run for the high ground, but there were laws against that, she thought with a momentary pang.

Leave it, Liz. Focus on the practical matter. Those musicians could all use the money.

"So," she began brightly, "you still want live music at the party?"

Jared nodded. "I still want music at the party," he confirmed.

"To show your sister that you won't be bossed around?" she guessed, smiling to herself.

He could have sworn he heard a smile in her voice. "To show my sister that she can be wrong at times," he corrected. "*And* to show her that I can be right once in a while."

Jared grinned, thinking of the woman he'd been getting together with. Because of her, he'd found himself looking forward to his evenings instead of staying late at the office and then coming home, drained and exhausted. She was like a second wind for him. A welcomed second wind.

"*Really* right," he emphasized.

Elizabeth didn't even try to ignore the strong, electrical jolt that insisted on shimmying up and down her spine in response to the warmth she heard in his voice. She decided—just this once—to just enjoy it.

She knew it wouldn't last.

Chapter Eight

"So who are these other musicians that you have in mind?" he asked Elizabeth, getting back to the business at hand.

"All very talented people who would round out the ensemble you had in mind rather nicely," she promised.

He knew that to appease Megan, he was going to have to audition these musicians, just as he had, in a way, Elizabeth audition for him.

"Would they be available to meet with me after hours?" he asked, then thought that maybe an explanation might be in order. "My time's a little limited from nine to five. I have this campaign due—"

"Campaign?" she repeated. What sort of a campaign? she wondered.

Political?

Or—?

It occurred to her that the only thing she knew about

Jared Winterset was that he made her pulse quicken when he looked at her a certain way and that he was apparently a good son and brother. And, hopefully, since he hadn't mentioned a wife, he wasn't married.

But, other than the fact that he was incredibly good-looking and kept making her mind wander into regions she didn't normally occupy, she knew nothing about what he did for a living—or anything personal for that matter. Maybe she should.

"Are you a politician?" she asked him suddenly.

"What?" For a second, he thought he'd misheard her. And then it dawned on him why she might think that. Because of the particular word he'd used. "Oh God, no." He laughed, unable to think of anything he would have disliked being more than that. "I'm in advertising. I was referring to an ad campaign I'm working on that's coming due. It's one of those things that requires burning the midnight oil and giving up a pint of blood along the way," he cracked.

"I see…" she said, feeling a bit silly.

"Anyway, are these musicians you mentioned available to meet with me after, say, six o'clock?" he asked tactfully, switching the subject.

She was about to say that they weren't available because they were working, then thought against it. What better opportunity for Jared to make up his mind if he liked what he heard than to *hear* them, just the way that he had heard her?

"As a matter of fact, this might just work out even better for everyone all around."

He wasn't sure what she was referring to, but he figured if he gave her enough time, she'd get around to explaining. "I'm listening."

"The people I thought of for your ensemble all happen to be playing with me tomorrow night in that production of *Fiddler on the Roof* at the Bedford playhouse. You know…the musical I mentioned to you the other evening? The one I'm leaving you a ticket for at the box office."

His brain felt so crowded with details lately, it took him a minute to remember what she was referring to. "Oh, right, you did mention that. Sorry, life's been a little crazy lately."

"No need to apologize, I know what it can be like. I have to write down all my different engagements or I'm liable to go to the wrong one—or forget to go altogether. So," she continued, "I'll be sure to leave that ticket in your name with the cashier at the box office. The performance starts at seven."

"I'll be there," he promised. And then a thought hit him. This would be a perfect opportunity to kill two birds with one stone. He couldn't have arranged this better if he'd tried. "Could you leave two tickets instead of one?" he asked. "I'll be more than happy to pay for both if there's a problem."

Two? The request for a second ticket left her feeling numb. That meant that there *was* someone, a wife, a girlfriend, someone who mattered in his life.

Elizabeth could feel her heart plummeting all the way down to her toes.

Idiot!

Well, what did she expect? A guy like Jared Winterset—successful, handsome, charming—wasn't exactly someone destined to die on the vine unnoticed. Hell, he probably had to sleep with a baseball bat next to him in order to beat back waves of women looking to find a man of substance.

"Sure. Two tickets. Done," she said, doing her best to retain the cheerful note in her voice.

But it was far from easy. All she could think of was that it was happening again. She was going to be providing the background music for someone else's romance. This time for a person she knew.

"And there's no need to pay for them. My invitation, my treat." The words were stuck in her throat and she didn't know how she was managing to get them out. "Now, if you'll excuse me, I have to get ready for rehearsal," she informed him crisply.

The line went dead before Jared got a chance to say goodbye.

Having preperformance jitters was nothing new for Elizabeth. She experienced it every single time she was slated to pick up her violin and play before an audience, no matter how large or small that audience was.

But this was something more.

This time she wasn't just having the typical jitters that quickly vanished the moment she struck the first chord. She was downright throwing-up-her-dinner nervous and it all had to do with the two empty, side-by-side seats in the third row. The ones located just off the aisle.

Those were the two seats corresponding to the two tickets she'd left with the cashier at the box office. The two tickets that were set aside for Jared and whoever it was who was accompanying him to the show tonight. Probably his girlfriend.

Oh c'mon, Liz. Get a grip.

She was making a mountain out of less than a mole-hill, she told herself. Just because Jared had asked for a second ticket didn't automatically mean he was bringing a significant other with him. Maybe he was the type who didn't like doing things alone and he was bringing a friend with him. A guy friend.

Or maybe his sister had returned from the cruise and he wanted her to hear for herself what the violinist he'd picked to play at their parents' party sounded like. Could she have really felt that there was *this* much chemistry going on between them if Jared was actually involved with another woman?

She didn't know.

Maybe he wasn't coming at all, she thought as she continued to look at the seats, which remained conspicuously empty.

She supposed that not having Jared come to the performance was better than seeing him come in with a female companion on his arm.

"Liz," Amanda Baker hissed from her seat in the pit, "why are you standing there like a lighthouse beacon, staring off into the theater? Sit down…it's almost time to start the overture."

Feeling self-conscious, Elizabeth glanced down at her friend. "Right."

Elizabeth sank down into her seat and then glanced over her shoulder for one last look at the audience before the houselights went down.

That was when she saw him.

Saw *them*.

Jared wasn't alone. He'd brought someone with him to fill the other seat.

A female someone.

An *unpregnant* female someone, Elizabeth realized, feeling a definite sharp prick in her heart that all but immobilized.

"Liz? Liz? *Elizabeth*," Amanda finally whispered urgently, resorting to her formal name in an attempt to get her attention. "What *is* it with you tonight?" she asked, concerned as well as just a little irritated.

She and Elizabeth had become practically inseparable over time and whatever was going on with Elizabeth, her friend was leaving her out of it. Amanda didn't like being kept in the dark.

Especially not by her best friend.

"Nothing. Nothing at all," Elizabeth all but snapped back. She turned around to face her sheet music. "Just a few more preperformance jitters than usual, that's all, Mandy."

"I don't believe you," Amanda retorted stubbornly. She shifted in her seat to look at the audience and was just in time to see the same couple that had brought on Elizabeth's deep, sad frown taking their seats. "Wow, now there's someone I'd definitely let ring my chimes." The moment she said that, enlightenment suddenly dawned on her. "You know him." It was more of a statement than a question.

If she lied, Amanda would eventually find out that she had, especially since she'd already mentioned to her and some of the others that Jared was looking for musicians to play at his parents' anniversary party and that in all likelihood, he would be attending the performance.

So, albeit very reluctantly, Elizabeth admitted to knowing him.

"Yes. He's the man I told you about, the one who's here to hear you, Nathan, Jack and Albert play so he can decide if he's going to hire you."

"Who's the chicklet with him?" Amanda wanted to know. Her dark eyes narrowed as she continued looking at the woman beside Jared.

Elizabeth managed to suppress the sigh that automatically rose up from her chest. "I have no idea."

Amanda read between the lines. "So then maybe it's not serious," she surmised. Her smile turned into a full-fledged grin. "Which means that that hunk is essentially free." She slanted a look at her friend as the houselights began to darken. "You're not interested in him, are you?"

"Me? No. Absolutely not," she denied a little too emphatically.

Amanda looked at her, a knowing smile spreading across her generous mouth. "Sorry, Liz, my mistake. I'm backing off."

"I said I wasn't interested in him," Elizabeth whispered harshly.

"Right." As the music swelled, her whisper grew just a tad louder. "You know…there's no shame in saying you're interested in the guy. Your heart would have to be made out of rocks not to be into a guy who looks like that. But if you decide to throw him over someday, don't forget who your best friend is." Amanda fluttered

her lashes at her in an exaggerated fashion. "I'm not too proud to accept your leftovers."

"He's not my leftover," Elizabeth insisted. "He's not my anything."

And he never will be.

Which was just as well, Elizabeth silently reminded herself. Love never turned out well anyway. Her parents had loved each other dearly. When her mother died suddenly, her father was utterly devastated. She could remember seeing the sadness in his eyes even though she'd been so young at the time.

If she didn't fall in love, she'd never have to endure the pain that came with loving someone.

"Denial doesn't become you," Amanda mouthed just as the music tempo began to increase.

The music, Liz, the music. Concentrate on the music. Nothing else matters except for the music. Elizabeth focused on her fingering and the sounds that emerged as she and her violin became one.

That was the only thing that really made sense. Music provided both order and solace in her life. It was what kept her grounded, no matter what. When her mother died, when the romance she thought she had disintegrated on her, it was music that had held her together and helped her deal with the pain of being left behind.

It was what she could always count on.

Music and her family.

Served her right for letting her imagination run away with her, she silently lectured as the overture began to wind down.

What on earth had she been thinking?

That was just the problem, Elizabeth realized. She hadn't been thinking, only reacting.

Well, she knew exactly where that sort of thing led, she thought.

Nowhere.

A beat later, she realized that the overture was over. Suppressing another sigh, she relaxed her hold on her violin and let the instrument rest.

Unlike her.

But for now, that was going to have to do.

"You played like you were on fire," Amanda whispered in complete awe. "Whatever you were channeling, keep it up."

She gave her best friend a spasmodic smile in response, then mentally retreated into a holding zone, waiting for the next number to come up, grateful for the low lighting that hid her flushed complexion.

Driven by a desire to block everything else out, Elizabeth threw herself into every number, playing her heart out and willing herself not to think of anything but the next notes that were coming up.

Mercifully, she managed to keep a very tight rein on herself.

And then it was over. The songs, the music, the play, it was all finished for the evening. And for the musical's run.

The cast, their hands linked together, forming a long human chain, took their bows a total of seven times as applause burst out over and over again, urging the performers to bow yet one more time.

Finally, the lead actor held up his hand to temporarily hold back the audience's applause. When he finally succeeded, he gestured toward the pit, indicating that the people who were seated there, comprising the orchestra, should all rise and take a well-deserved bow as well.

When everyone stood up around her, turning to face the audience now that the houselights were up, Elizabeth had no choice but to stand up as well. If she didn't, she knew that she'd be too conspicuous and draw the very attention she was trying to avoid.

This way, she hoped she would be able to merge with the other musicians.

But the moment she turned around, Elizabeth couldn't help looking in Jared's direction. Part of her couldn't help wondering if he was even still there, or if he'd decided to leave and find someplace more private for himself and the redhead he'd brought with him.

He was still there, in the seat she'd gotten for him.

What was more, he was actually making eye contact with her. When he saw her looking his way, he grinned and gave her a thumbs-up, just before he started clapping again.

After a couple of minutes and one final curtain call, the cast began to disperse. The moment they started to move off the stage, the members of the orchestra began to file out of the pit as well.

And then, to her horror, she saw Jared making his way toward the front—toward her. The woman he'd brought to the performance was right behind him. He was holding her hand so they wouldn't get separated.

Terrific, he was bringing up his girlfriend for her to meet.

Bracing herself, Elizabeth put on her best professional-violinist smile and inclined her head in a silent greeting.

"You were fantastic!" Jared burst out the moment he was close enough for her to be able to hear him.

Elizabeth politely murmured, "Thank you."

Jared looked at her, puzzled at her lack of exuberance, wondering if he'd said something wrong, or had unwittingly crossed some line—literally—that he wasn't supposed to.

"You really were," the woman beside him said with feeling. "It was wonderful. Magical," she corrected. "It was so professional sounding."

"Well, it's not as if this was our first time," Elizabeth answered.

The moment the words were out, it hit her that she was sounding a bit catty. She softened her initial statement by adding, "Most of us play as much as we can manage. This theater group alone does several different musicals a year and a lot of us get called back for all of them."

"Well, I was just in heaven the entire time," the woman told her, completely uninhibited and obviously thrilled to have had this evening out. She turned toward Jared and formally issued her thanks. "I'm glad you didn't listen to me and forced me into coming with you."

"I always told you I know best," Jared responded with a smile that was far too familiar for Elizabeth to bear seeing.

She turned abruptly away. "Well, if you'll excuse me, I've got to pack up—"

Had he misunderstood her when they'd talked yesterday?

"Wait, didn't you say that you wanted me to meet some of the musicians?" he reminded her.

"I did, but it can wait until another time." Her mouth as well as her cheeks were beginning to ache as she continued to maintain the smile on her lips. A smile that only went down as far as her facial muscles. She certainly didn't *feel* like smiling. "After all, you don't want your date to get bored, meeting a bunch of musicians," she pointed out.

"Date?" Jared echoed, staring at her and completely confused as to what she was referring to. "You think this is my *date?*"

And then, as he realized the mistake, he laughed. Really laughed. Hard.

The redhead beside him looked as if she was somewhat offended by his reaction. "It's not *that* funny, Jared," she protested.

"Oh, yes, it is," he contradicted, despite the fact that there was obvious affection in his voice.

The grin spreading out on his face made him appear even more boyish than he already looked. And then, as his laughter subsided, he realized that he was to blame for the apparent misunderstanding. Caught up in the moment and thoroughly enjoying himself tonight, he'd forgotten to do one important thing.

This time his expression was a bit sheepish as he looked at Elizabeth.

"I didn't introduce the two of you to each other, did I?"

"No, you didn't," both Elizabeth and the woman standing beside him said at the exact same moment.

Chapter Nine

"No time like the present," Jared said, then quickly tried to remedy the situation by making the heretofore overlooked introductions. "Elizabeth Stephens, I'd like you to meet Julie Lyle—my cousin," he tacked on.

"Your *cousin*," Elizabeth repeated, torn between feeling like an idiot and wanting to do a little dance in the orchestra pit. She managed to block the former and refrain from the latter, but she couldn't suppress the wide smile of relief that rose to her lips.

"My cousin," he confirmed, then turning toward his female companion, he brought the introduction full circle. "Julie, this is Elizabeth, the woman who's going to bring music into my parents' lives by playing at their anniversary celebration."

"Hi. I have a confession to make." Julie's expression was genuine and warm as she shook Elizabeth's hand. "When Jared invited me to come listen to you, my first reaction was to beg off. I'm not what you might call a big musical buff and things haven't exactly been going well lately. All I wanted to do was stay home and feel sorry for myself. But Jared refused to take no for an answer." She flashed him an appreciative grin. "He's as much of a pain in the neck now as he was when we were growing up. Never took no for an answer then, either."

Jared addressed his defense to Elizabeth rather than answering his cousin directly. "I prefer thinking of myself as being persuasive."

Julie hooked her arms through one of his. "Well, whatever you want to call it, I'm glad you bullied me into coming because I *thoroughly* enjoyed myself tonight," she said enthusiastically, looking at Elizabeth as she declared the last part, then confided, "It's been a long time since I've been able to say that."

Although that had decidedly aroused her curiosity, Elizabeth held her tongue. She didn't know Jared's cousin well enough to ask *why* she hadn't been able to enjoy herself for a long time.

As if reading her mind, Jared answered her silent question. "Julie's husband is in the National Guard and he was called up two months ago. For the last month, he's been deployed overseas."

"Which has officially been the longest month of my life," the redhead lamented. Her words were accompanied by a long, deep sigh. "But thanks to Jared's pestering, I forgot to be worried for a couple of hours. I know you probably hear this all the time, but you play beautifully."

Elizabeth knew that there was no way the woman could have distinguished her playing from that of the rest of the orchestra, or, at the very least, from the other violinists, but she accepted the enthusiastic compliment graciously.

"I never grow tired of hearing kind words about my playing." Her eyes crinkled at the corners as she smiled at the other woman. "I'm very glad that you enjoyed the performance."

Jared looked on as the two women talked. He was feeling rather proud of himself. It had been no easy feat getting Julie out of her house and away from the darker thoughts that insisted on preying upon her mind, but he'd managed to accomplish his mission.

With any luck, Derek, Julie's husband, would return to the States unharmed. Even if for some awful reason, he didn't, having Julie worry herself sick was not going to change the ultimate outcome one iota, or help her get through it.

By getting her to accompany him to the play, he'd not only done a good deed, but he also had gotten himself a second opinion about Elizabeth. He had to admit he wasn't exactly all that impartial when it came to Elizabeth's playing. His heart had been in his throat when he'd watched the stunning blonde with the gifted fingers and beautiful blue eyes perform onstage. Truth was, his reaction to this woman was getting in the way of his reaction to her music. He was a fair enough man to know that he needed a second opinion to fall back on, and in case Megan gave him a hard time about choosing Elizabeth, one to support his own.

He knew for a fact that Megan would ask to interview Elizabeth herself the moment her cruise ship docked. It was always good to be one jump ahead of his sister when it came to something like this.

"So, about these people you wanted me to meet…" Jared prodded, awaiting a response from Elizabeth.

It amazed Elizabeth to no end just how buoyed she could feel after being so incredibly low just a couple of minutes ago. She tried not to think about what that actually meant in the long run and focused exclusively on the question that Jared had just asked. She needed to have him meet the musicians she thought would round out the ensemble.

"They're close by," she told him brightly. "I told them about the kind of music that was going to be played, as well as the time and date for the celebration. They're all free that evening and they've all been playing professionally for years," she informed him.

With each word she uttered, she was feeling more and more energized, as if she'd just gotten a fresh shot of adrenaline—and, in a way, she had.

"As a matter of fact, I can have them play a sample number for you right now if you'd like so you can hear for yourself what the program you put together for the celebration would sound like."

"The program *we* put together," Jared corrected, but even that wasn't entirely accurate. For the most part, the program was actually largely *her* doing. He'd merely nodded his head whenever she made a suggestion, finding that she had very good instincts when it came to setting up the musical playlist. Each song she'd mentioned turned out to be another song he recalled one or both of his parents favoring when he was growing up.

When she made her suggestion about listening to a

sample repertoire, he was about to say that he thought that was why she'd invited him to attend the play in the first place—so he could hear the ensemble perform together. But he was beginning to discover that with Elizabeth, there was no such thing as taking a breath before answering. In the time it took to draw that breath, she was already moving on. In this case, she was already beckoning over several musicians who were hanging back on the far side of the orchestra pit. It was obvious that they were waiting to be introduced.

As they crossed over to her, Elizabeth rattled off their names, saying them so quickly that Jared found he'd missed most of them. Before he could ask to have their names repeated, the players were already taking their places.

And then they began to perform a short rock-and-roll medley Elizabeth had prepared ahead of time. Jared caught himself tapping his foot in time to the beat. If this was a preview of things to come, his parents were going to love it.

Stepping back to stand next to his cousin, Jared saw by the expression on Julie's face that she agreed with his assessment.

Elizabeth and the ensemble she'd selected wound up playing for ten minutes, incorporating among other songs a ballad and a number that brought to mind everything that the words *rock and roll* stood for.

When they finished, Julie broke into enthusiastic applause. Prompted by the sound of her clapping, Jared joined in, nodding his head in hearty approval. This was going to turn out to be even better than he had initially hoped for.

"Fantastic," he pronounced. He was rather amazed that these folks hadn't forged singular professional careers for themselves, the kind of careers that brought accolades as well as substantial monetary rewards with them. "You've certainly convinced me," he said, his eyes sweeping over the entire group.

Amanda was the first to speak, looking from Jared to Elizabeth. "So we're hired?" She evidently wanted to hear one of them say the actual words.

"You're definitely hired," Jared told her, then nodded at the others in the ensemble.

Julie, ever practical, tugged on his arm to get his attention. When Jared looked in her direction, raising a questioning brow, she said in a lower voice, "Shouldn't you discuss their fees with them first?"

"I left all that to Elizabeth," he answered, looking over Julie's head to the other woman. Actually, he and Elizabeth had come to an agreement in their negotiations. The fee she'd asked for had been somewhat lower than he'd expected so he readily agreed to pay it. "Right?" he asked the beautiful blonde.

On the surface, there was nothing remotely intimate about the exchange, yet she felt this warm tingle when he looked in her direction for confirmation. For just that second, it was as if there were only the two of them engaged in a private conversation.

"Right." She turned toward the others, incredibly pleased with the way everything had ultimately turned out. "I'll be in touch with all the sheet music you'll need," she promised. "And I'll let you know when we're getting together for rehearsals."

"Sounds good to me," Jack Borman, the keyboard artist, told her.

Nathan, who played the cello, rubber-stamped the approval. "Same here."

Albert, who had never met an instrument he couldn't play, but favored timpani drums, paused to shake Jared's hand and thank him before he, too, left the pit.

Amanda was the last of the selected group to go, lingering as long as she could, trying hard not to be overly obvious that she was scrutinizing Jared up close and personal.

When he did look in her direction, she was quick to cover her actions. "I just wanted to say thanks a lot for the gig. I always liked the oldies," she added for good measure.

Elizabeth caught herself just in time. She had almost interrupted her best friend, saying that no, she didn't. Amanda preferred classical music and made a point of letting people know she felt almost everything else ran a distant second.

But she knew that Amanda wouldn't appreciate being called on the carpet like that. So Elizabeth remained silent, waiting for the other woman to finish.

When she did, Amanda nodded at her and said cheerfully, "I'll see you later."

Then, turning so that she was only facing her and had her back to Jared and his cousin, Amanda moved her eyes in an exaggerated fashion, indicating that she thought Elizabeth should make some sort of a play for the tall, handsome man before someone else snatched him up.

Elizabeth pointedly ignored Amanda's efforts.

The latter left, making no effort to suppress the sigh that escaped her lips. That, too, Elizabeth ignored, or at least tried to.

Instead, she briefly turned her attention toward Jared.

"Thanks again for coming," she told him with feeling. "To be honest, I didn't know if you would or not." *But I was hoping you would.*

"I'm not very big on musicals," he confessed freely. He and Julie had that in common, he thought. "But I have to admit, I've always liked *Fiddler.* There's just something about that play that makes it really enjoyable."

He wasn't alone in his reaction. "A lot of people have said that," Elizabeth told him. "It's probably the main reason there have been so many revivals of the play."

As she talked, she packed her instrument into the case she had left tucked under her seat. She didn't want to appear as if she was finding reasons to linger. The last thing she needed was to come across as someone who didn't know when to go home.

Snapping the locks into place, she said, "Well, I'll be seeing you." She nodded politely at Julie, then told Jared, "If there's anything else you can think of that you need—for the celebration," she tacked on in case he thought she was issuing him another sort of invitation, "please don't hesitate to call me."

As she turned to go, Jared realized that he didn't want her leaving just yet. He was as surprised as she was to hear himself saying, "Julie and I are going out for coffee and maybe some dessert."

"What do you mean, 'maybe'? Dessert's the good part. I can skip the coffee," Julie told him.

"She's a walking sweet tooth," he confided to Elizabeth. "Would you like to join us?" he asked, then, in case she felt uncomfortable about turning him down, he gave her a way out. "Unless you've already made other plans...."

"No, no other plans," she assured him quickly, then smiled at the invitation. "Coffee and cake sound really wonderful. Where are we going?"

"Not far," he assured her. "There's a little French bakery located about half a mile or so from here. It has outdoor seating so that you can have your coffee and dessert under the stars."

It sounded absolutely perfect, but she would have been just as willing to have bread and water in the middle of an open field, as long as she was sharing both with him.

She knew she was letting herself get carried away, but by the same token, she'd already accepted the fact that it was her fate not to have any sort of a meaningful relationship for any real duration of time. What was happening right now came under the heading of "two ships passing in the night" and that was okay with her. And who knew? Maybe she'd get lucky and the ships would pass each other slowly.

So she smiled at Jared and said in response to his summation, "What more can a person ask for?"

Their eyes met and held for a long moment. And then he murmured, "Beats me," despite the fact that what he would have asked for—had he had the opportunity— was to have that coffee and dessert with her *without* his cousin being in the picture. But he couldn't very well tell Julie to find her own way home, especially not after he'd worked so hard to get her *out* of the house.

"I can give you a ride there," he offered Elizabeth. "And then drive you back here to your car later."

Much as she would have liked that, it wasn't really practical, so she waved away the offer. "Too complicated, with you having to do too much driving back and forth," she told him. "I'll just follow you," she said. "And in case I lose you, I'd better get the address."

"I don't know the address," he admitted with a careless shrug. "I just go by instinct."

Julie just shook her head. "Spoken like a typical man," she said, then turned toward Elizabeth. "*I* know the address." And then she proceeded to recite it for Elizabeth's benefit.

The latter jotted it down quickly on the notepad she'd pulled out of her purse.

"Got it," she declared, slipping pen and pad back into her purse. "Thanks," she said to the redhead, then promised Jared, "I'll be right behind you."

He recalled the last time they were both heading toward one destination. "No, you won't. You'll probably be there long before we are."

"But it's close by," Julie pointed out as she followed him out to his car. The night slipped around them like a soft, black suede glove.

"Trust me," he told her, getting in behind the steering wheel. "She'll find a way to be there a lot sooner than we will."

Elizabeth said nothing, but she secretly liked the fact that what he'd just said was meant to tease her.

* * *

"I never realized that there were so many details that had to be looked into and taken care of," Jared commented later that evening, as he, his cousin and Elizabeth sat, enjoying their steaming mugs of gourmet coffee.

"Really?" Elizabeth asked curiously.

"Yes…really. When I was in college and someone threw a party, they called the local deli or the sandwich shop and put in an order for one or two huge sandwiches. Someone else would take care of getting the keg of beer. The people coming to the party brought their own chips and dip and whatever else they wanted to eat. Invitations went out by word of mouth, usually the day of the party, and just like that—" he snapped his fingers "—violà, you had a party.

"This," he said with a sigh, referring to the anniversary celebration, "is way too involved and complicated. It's not fun anymore," he added for good measure.

"You could have gotten a party planner," Elizabeth suggested.

"I did," he told her. When she raised a quizzical eyebrow, he said, "My sister, who put together this endless list, browbeat me into promising I'd follow everything to the letter and then promptly sailed away—literally," he complained.

"Oh, it's not that bad, Jared." Julie laughed. "You've got a caterer handling the food. You've already rented the hall and you've just finished making arrangements for the music," she summed up, slanting a glance, as well as a smile, in Elizabeth's direction. "Sounds like all of it's being handled if you ask me."

Just to prove Julie wrong, Jared gave her the highlights of one of his ship-to-shore calls from his sister. "Megan called and asked what flower arrangements I'd picked out. I asked what flowers. She answered, the flowers the florist showed you. At which point I asked—"

"What florist?" Elizabeth guessed. Her intuition earned her a laugh from both Jared and his cousin.

"So you understand," Jared said, feeling vindicated.

Much as she would have liked reinforcing his assumption, she couldn't. She wouldn't have been able to utter a lie even if it was burning on her tongue.

"It's not so much that I understand," she explained, "as I have brothers."

It took him a second to puzzle her words out. "So you're saying it's a guy thing?"

"Most definitely," Elizabeth told him with unwavering sincerity. "You're all about shortcuts and we're all about details." She caught Julie's eye and the other woman nodded her agreement.

The silent communication was not lost on Jared. "Hey, you're ganging up on me. Two against one, no fair," he pretended to protest.

"It's only not fair if we're wrong," Elizabeth pointed out.

He felt as if he'd just been snowed. "Who made that rule up?" he wanted to know with a laugh.

Elizabeth shrugged her shoulders dismissively. "It slipped my mind."

He had his answer right there. "That's undoubtedly because you're the one who made it up," he said with a laugh. "Just for that, you don't get any seconds on the cake."

Julie leaned forward and said to her newfound friend in what amounted to a stage whisper, "I'd steer clear of him if I were you, Elizabeth. My cousin has always been a very sore loser."

"Thanks for the warning, but I can take care of myself."

"I bet you can."

The comment came from Jared, not his cousin. The look on his face was utterly unreadable.

Now, what was that supposed to mean? Elizabeth wondered. Was it a good thing, or a bad thing?

Men, she was completely convinced, really should come with some sort of a handbook, preferably a user-friendly one.

Chapter Ten

It was, Elizabeth decided, like living in a dream.

Or maybe one of those old-fashioned romantic comedies from decades past, the ones where the hero never needed a shave and the heroine would wake up with every hair in place and a dewy face that never required having makeup reapplied.

Whatever she was currently experiencing certainly didn't even remotely approximate her usual frantic but basically bland day-to-day life. Ever since this mysterious "Mrs. Manetti" had sent Jared Winterset her way, life had gone from fairly decent to absolutely perfect.

Oh, she and Jared weren't actually dating or anything like that, but perforce, they *were* seeing one another just about every evening. She found herself *living* for the evenings.

And when they weren't seeing each other, they were talking on the phone. Either Jared was calling her about another song he remembered or she was calling him about a different rendition that had just occurred to her for one of the songs they'd already selected.

For Elizabeth, music had always been her passion; performing it defined her very life. And for a very limited amount of time, this handsome, intelligent and exceedingly sensual man was sharing this world with her.

It really didn't get much better than that.

"What do you mean it doesn't get any better than that?" Amanda wanted to know when she'd finally cornered her friend and gotten Elizabeth to tell her a little about what was happening between her and Jared.

They'd just finished rehearsing. Amanda had hung back, waiting for the others to leave. She was practically chomping at the bit to quiz Elizabeth about her progress with Mr. Too-Good-Looking-for-Words, which was the way she whimsically referred to Jared.

"Has he kissed you yet?" Amanda prodded.

"Well, no, but…" Elizabeth began, trying not to sound as breathless as visions of kissing Jared had rendered her. She didn't get a chance to finish because Amanda was rolling her eyes, looking to heaven for strength.

"*That's* how it gets 'better than that,'" she declared in exasperation. "Damn, girl, you're probably wearing those nice and tidy little Ms. Professional outfits of yours when you see him." Amanda continued staring at her, waiting for an answer. "Am I right?"

Instead of answering, Elizabeth went on the defensive. "What's wrong with my clothes?"

"I'm right." Amanda's words were accompanied by

a weary sigh. "Liz, Liz, Liz, I am *really* going to have to take you under my wing, here."

Elizabeth shook her head. She really liked Amanda, but there was no way she wanted to be turned into a carbon copy of her. "I really don't think that's such a good idea."

"No, it's not," she agreed, then, in case Elizabeth thought she'd won, Amanda clarified what she meant. "It's a *great* idea. Honey, you want this man to keep turning up even *after* the party's over, don't you?"

She refused to have any expectations. As long as she accepted the fact that what was going on between them had a limited life expectancy, she wasn't setting herself up for a fall. She knew that her best friend didn't think that way, but Amanda was a lot more resilient than she was in that department. Her pal fell in and out of love with the regularity of a sunrise.

Elizabeth had a feeling that she took after her father when it came to romance. If she fell in love, it would be forever. Consequently, she really couldn't let her guard down, couldn't afford to allow herself to fall for Jared, no matter *how* much her heart yearned for him. The risks involved were just too great.

"Well, that would be nice," Elizabeth hedged, not wanting to get into any complicated explanations about why she actually didn't want any long-term relationship. "But—"

"You can show *that* off, too," Amanda assured her. "For a girl who doesn't work out, you've got a very nice derriere, but first we're going to capture him using your frontal assets, so to speak." She smiled broadly at her adroit imagery.

"I'd really rather that you *didn't* speak," Elizabeth told her, but even as she made her request, she knew it was falling on deaf ears. Once Amanda became focused on a goal, God help the world.

Now, apparently, was no different.

"Tough. I can't just stand by on the sidelines and watch you toss away what is clearly the opportunity of a lifetime." She saw Elizabeth about to protest and talked more rapidly. "Oh, I know that they say you have all the time in the world and there are dozens of matches for each and every person, but hell," she declared with feeling, waving away the previous statement, "it's a really big world and you and your perfect mate may *never* get together."

Elizabeth was trying her best not to show her impatience. "And your point is…?"

"My point is that when fate hits you over the head with the opportunity of a lifetime, you don't just shake it off and keep walking. And, in case you haven't noticed, Liz, fate all but pushed this man into your life." Amanda gave her a penetrating look. "Now *do* something about it."

"I am," Elizabeth insisted. "I'm giving him more than his money's worth."

She could see by the light that had just come into Amanda's eyes that the woman was *not* interpreting her response the right way. She was quick to set her friend straight.

"I usually charge a higher rate per hour, but since he's also hiring you and the others I recommended for this ensemble—plus he put himself out to fix my car that evening it died in the studio parking lot—I decided it was only fair to lower my rates."

But Amanda shook her head. "You're talking about business. *I'm* talking about pleasure."

Elizabeth lifted one shoulder in a vague shrug. Yes, she and Jared were getting along well, and she thought that there might even be a strong possibility that he was interested in her. But it was only temporary. This was definitely nothing to build her hopes on. Besides, that route only led to greater disappointment.

"Pleasure's not the point," she told Amanda evasively.

Her friend just pushed harder. "You're wrong, Liz. Pleasure is the *only* point. It's what makes the music in you happen. Now, we're about the same size, and I've got this really slinky dress—"

It took Elizabeth only a minute to realize which dress Amanda was talking about. "You mean the one that looks like someone stitched five small handkerchiefs together?"

"Four," Amanda corrected, clearly getting a kick out of the description. "That's the one. Why don't you wear it tonight?" she prodded, then looked at her knowingly. "I'm assuming that the two of you are getting together tonight, seeing as how the anniversary celebration is not all that far off now."

"Jared did mention something about stopping by…" Elizabeth said vaguely. She didn't quite pull off the disinterested pose she was trying for.

"Your place, huh?" Amanda paused significantly, then asked, "Have you been to his, yet?"

"No…I—" And then she realized where Amanda

was going with this. Closing her violin case, she snapped the locks and picked the case up, more than ready to leave. "He doesn't have a wife, Mandy."

Amanda fell into step beside her. "How do you know for sure?"

There was no way around this one, she thought. Lying, cleverly or otherwise, had never been her strong suit. She knew she was leaving herself open with what she was about to admit, but she really didn't have a choice. "I looked him up."

Amanda's eyes sparkled and her grin was practically blinding. "Aha!"

"No 'aha,'" Elizabeth insisted archly. "I was just curious about him—" That admission, she realized, just got her in deeper.

The expression on Amanda's face said she knew exactly why she had gone trolling through the internet. To prove her point, she asked innocently, "Did you ever look up Mr. Tannenbaum?"

That was the name of the man who had hired them to play at another playhouse last fall. "No, but—"

"And the fact that Mr. Tannenbaum looked like a lizard having a bad hair day had nothing to do with it, right?" Amanda pressed, not bothering to hide the triumphant smirk on her lips.

"No, it didn't," Elizabeth fired back, knowing that she had already lost this round.

Amanda patted her shoulder. "You just keep on telling yourself that, girl. And in the meantime, follow me to my apartment and take the dress," she urged.

She knew Amanda. She was going to continue pushing this dress on her every time they were within hearing range of each other. "You're not going to give me any peace until I do, are you?"

Amanda grinned, knowing she'd won. "Nope."

"Okay, I'll follow you home, and you can give me the dress."

Amanda eyed her suspiciously. "Promise you'll wear it."

Elizabeth suppressed a sigh. "I'll wear it."

"Around Jared when he's in your house?"

Amanda knew her too well. Enough was enough, Elizabeth thought. "Mandy—"

"Say it," Amanda pressed. "I know you. If you say it, you'll have to do it. Otherwise, you'll be lying to me and Elizabeth Stephens doesn't lie."

God, but she made her sound so boring, Elizabeth thought. Was she really that predictable? "Amanda, he's going to think I'm trying to seduce him."

"And why's that a bad thing?" Amanda purred. "Now, c'mon, swear to me that you'll wear the dress around Jared." She caught Elizabeth's hand, holding her hostage. "I'm not letting you go anywhere until you say it," she warned.

Anything to get this over with, Elizabeth thought. "I'll take the dress, and wear it around Jared Winterset. Happy?"

Amanda released her hand and grinned widely. "Very."

Elizabeth shot her a dark look as they reached her car. "Well, I'm not."

"But you will be," Amanda promised with a wicked grin. "With just the tiniest bit of luck, Lizzie, you will be."

* * *

"Wow."

Jared stood stone still in Elizabeth's doorway, suddenly finding himself in the clutches of temporary memory loss.

More simply put, he'd forgotten how to walk. Not only that but he had to remind himself—after his chest all but imploded—how to breathe.

He'd thought of Elizabeth as being exceptionally lovely from the moment he'd first seen her on the studio soundstage, surrounded by other musicians, but definitely in a class by herself. This, however, was a whole new level of attraction he was experiencing. The woman was downright gorgeous with physical attributes he hadn't been conscious of until just now.

Actually, in view of her present appearance, he decided that he must have been relatively unconscious prior to this moment.

The light blue spandex dress brought out her eyes and showcased her curves, making him damn glad to be alive and a man.

"That is *really* one sensational dress," he told her after he'd found his tongue again and had miraculously regained the ability to move his feet so that he could finally make it over the threshold.

"Thank you," she murmured. There was no denying that she felt rather self-conscious in this abbreviated dress she had on—but she had to admit that she really liked the way he was looking at her: as if she were a woman, not just a violinist. "It's not mine," she heard herself blurting out.

That was her, she thought almost in despair, honest to a fault.

"You stole it?" Jared teased.

"No, I mean it's Amanda's." Appalled at herself for the admission, she felt herself sinking further and further into the mire without having her feet touch bottom. "She seemed to think that I should wear it."

He couldn't take his eyes off her. "Remind me to send Amanda a thank-you note," he murmured. "She has excellent taste. You sure this belongs to her? The dress looks like it was made for you."

Elizabeth turned to face him, the dress whispering along her hips as she moved. He felt his gut tightening in a way that had nothing to do with anniversary parties or music—except, perhaps, the kind that two people might make when they were alone.

She lifted her shoulders in what was supposed to be a careless shrug, but the movement caused the straps on either side of the dress to slide down her shoulders almost at the same time.

As he watched the twin pieces of material sink seductively down the slopes of creamy-white shoulders, Jared felt his gut tightening even harder. Tightening so hard that for a moment, he thought he was going to need an oxygen mask.

Her self-consciousness increasing a hundredfold, Elizabeth pushed the errant straps back up where they belonged and murmured, "I'm just going to go upstairs and change into something a little more me—"

But as she started to turn away, she felt Jared catch hold of her arm.

"Why don't you do that later?" he said huskily. "I

don't have much time and I'll have even less if you go and change. I mean, changing takes time and—"

This was just not coming out right at all, Jared silently upbraided himself. Since when did he come off like some ungainly teenager? He'd never thought of himself as being this suave lady killer, but he certainly wasn't some fumbling dolt, either. He'd never lacked for female companionship and talking to the fairer sex had never been a problem for him, not since the moment he'd learned how to string five words together.

Moreover, in his professional life, talking was his lifeline and he did it with flair and aplomb. So what was it about this woman that seemed to throw all his skills out the window?

Granted, Elizabeth was bright and vivacious, but she certainly wasn't a femme fatale. And he was no simple-minded bumpkin.

So why did he sound like one?

"That's okay, I'll be really fast," she promised.

This dress really wasn't her and the longer she had it on, the more alien it felt on her. She felt as if she were pretending to be something she wasn't, trying to sell a product that had nothing to back it up.

"All I have to do—" In her hurry to make her escape as quickly as possible, somehow she managed to bump into him and wound up making contact so hard she accidentally threw herself off balance.

A flash of embarrassment shot through her, along with the realization that she was going to fall right at his feet.

As if she hadn't humiliated herself enough already. But just when she was certain that she was going to wind up sprawled out in front of him, Jared came to her rescue, just as he had that first night in the studio parking lot. He caught her before she ever came close to making contact with the floor.

He managed to keep her upright by pulling her up so close against his own torso that he could actually feel the tempo of her rapid heartbeat.

As she savored the sensation of their bodies fitting together so succinctly, it felt as if a bolt of lightning had struck him.

Several bolts, actually.

He certainly felt a jolt going through his entire body, momentarily wiping out his mind.

That would have been as good an explanation as any why he did what he did next. Why one second he was just focused on catching her, the next he'd branched out and found himself capturing her lips with his own.

He honestly could not recall, when he tried to go over it step-by-step later, how he'd seamlessly gone from catching to kissing, but he had.

And the second he had, his entire biological composition seemed to change. From rugged he-man to a towering mass of feelings, emotions and very hot responses.

She made his head spin, his blood rush, and myriad other scintillating reactions were also swirling through him, born in the fire of this completely unplanned kiss.

Without thinking—he really *couldn't* think—Jared tightened his arms around her and deepened the kiss that was already sending him in a free fall down into the mouth of a fiery volcano.

When his brain finally managed to reconnect again,

the thought "this was crazy" telegraphed itself through it over and over again.

It might be crazy, but he didn't care. Whatever he was going to have to do at a later date to make amends for this blatant transgression, it was worth it. Really worth it.

Especially when he felt her kiss him back.

Thank you, Amanda. I owe you. I owe you big-time! Elizabeth thought even as the shock of what she was doing penetrated.

Had *he* initiated this kiss or had *she?*

She honestly didn't know.

Elizabeth felt her toes curling and her inner core tingling the way she *knew* she'd never felt before.

Any second now, he was going to stop, but until he did…she was going to enjoy this incredible sensation for all she was worth.

Because this was far better than anything she could have ever imagined.

He made the entire world disappear until there was nothing left of it.

Nothing except for this fiery kiss.

Elizabeth rose a little higher on her toes and disappeared into the kiss a little further.

There were even bells ringing.

Insistently.

Chapter Eleven

At first Jared thought he was just imagining it. He couldn't be hearing bells.

But he was, because there it was again.

Strange, high-pitched bells.

And then, as the ring continued, tearing holes in the rising sense of euphoria that was embracing him, Jared realized that he wasn't imagining things. The sound was real.

And very close by.

His pocket.

The ringing was coming from his pocket.

Then suddenly it dawned on him, clearing away the smoldering haze. Those weren't bells he was hearing ring, that was his cell phone.

He stifled an inward groan. Talk about awful timing. For a split second, he debated ignoring the call, but even as he wavered in his resolve, Elizabeth was already withdrawing, taking a step back from him.

The moment had ended.

He forced himself to look into her eyes, to see if he could detect any signs of either anger or shock. Both were absent, but there *was* a strange look on her face, one he couldn't read.

"Elizabeth—" he began, not knowing just what he was going to say. He was spared the indecision. She cut him off.

"You'd better answer that. Whoever it is is obviously anxious to talk to you," she surmised since the cycle had already repeated itself three times. The cell phone would ring four times, then whoever was calling obviously hung up when Jared's voice mail kicked in, only to immediately call again, beginning the whole process all over again.

"Yeah, you're right," he reluctantly agreed. Resigned, he pulled his phone out of his pocket, pressed the green band enabling him to take the call and blew out a long breath, "Hello?"

Even as he placed the phone against his ear, he dragged his free hand through his hair, as if that would somehow help him pull himself together and wipe the fog from his brain. His brain was taking its own sweet time to reengage.

He honestly couldn't remember a kiss *ever* doing that to him, ever making him feel as if he were trying to remain upright as he stood at the epicenter of a 9.5 earthquake.

"Jared? Is that you? You sound strange, dear. Are you all right?"

He recognized the voice instantly. His mother was on the other end of the line.

Of all the times for her to call…

"I'm fine, Mom." As if by reflex, he slanted a glance at Elizabeth. She looked somewhat flustered that the caller who had interrupted their kiss was his mother. "You just caught me in the middle of something."

"Oh?" He could tell by her tone that he'd made a mistake. His mother sounded instantly intrigued. "Anything interesting?"

He decided that maybe it wasn't such a good idea to look at Elizabeth as he tried to regain his footing on a foundation in the midst of liquefaction.

"It could have been," he said, more to himself than to answer his mother's question.

"Well, I'll be quick," his mother promised, "and then you can go back to your project."

He laughed shortly. "Not exactly an option, Mom." After all, he wasn't about to drag Elizabeth back into his arms, flippantly muttering something along the lines of "Where were we?" before he locked lips with her again. No, this was an opportunity that had slipped through his fingers.

Maybe it was all for the best at that. He'd never felt this disoriented before from just a mere kiss. "Go ahead, Mom. What can I do for you?"

"You can tell me that you'll come by and feed Mrs. Mittens for me."

He became instantly alert as an uneasy suspicion began to creep through him. He noticed the inquisitive look on Elizabeth's face, and then realized that he'd accidentally hit the speaker button on his cell. Elizabeth had heard, too.

"Why am I feeding Mrs. Mittens?" he wanted to know, hoping his suspicions were wrong. He took the phone off Speaker again. "Why aren't you feeding her?"

"Really, dear, I would have thought you would have put two and two together by now. Because I won't be here," she explained. "Your father and I are going away for a couple of days."

He saw his plans begin to fall apart, leaving him with a choice he would have rather not had to make, especially since either way could lead to disaster. "What do you mean you won't be here? Where are you going?"

"Just down to San Diego, to this lovely little bed-and-breakfast." He could hear the smile in his mother's voice. "Your father's taking me there for our anniversary. You know, I think this is the first time we're actually going somewhere that didn't involve travel for his work since—well, since our honeymoon," his mother said. "Needless to say, we are *long* overdue."

Jared had turned off Speaker, but whatever was going on, it couldn't be good, Elizabeth thought. He looked almost stricken. She listened more intently as she did her best to fill in the blanks. Nothing she came up with was very promising.

"But you can't go, Mom," Jared protested, searching for a way to get his parents to remain in town without being forced to tell her about the anniversary celebration. Making it a surprise had been Megan's idea and he hadn't been happy about that from the start. Now he knew why.

"Oh, but we finally are," his mother contradicted, brimming with anticipation.

His mind went in four different directions at once, searching for a plausible excuse that would convince his mother and father to stay in town for their anniversary.

Glancing toward Elizabeth, he continued searching for at least a glimmer of an idea.

All he came up with was a shred of a glimmer. "Well, I guess I'll just have to tell you. Megan and I were planning on taking you out for your anniversary."

"You can still take us out, dear," his mother assured him. "Just after the fact—or even before the big day if you'd rather—provided your sister gets back in time, of course. Really, a cruise when she's six months pregnant?" She clucked in obvious disapproval. "*Not* a good idea."

She'd heard enough on Jared's end to piece together what was happening—and what he was trying to accomplish. An idea came to her, sparked by the soul-searing kiss they'd just shared.

Elizabeth looked around for something to write with as well as something to write on. Spying the back of a discarded envelope containing an application for a gym membership she had no interest in, she grabbed it and quickly wrote on it in block letters.

Convinced this would do the trick and get his mother to stay in Bedford, she held the envelope up in front of Jared.

When he didn't look at it at first, she tugged on his arm to get his attention, then pointed urgently to the message she'd just written.

Distracted, still looking for a way to temporarily

abort his mother's plans for a getaway, he glanced at the message on the envelope.

Stunned didn't even begin to describe how he felt. But as he reread the message, he decided that Elizabeth's idea just might work.

"Um, I'll have something important to tell you at that dinner." Clearing his throat, he continued a bit more confidently. "There's someone I want to introduce you to and I thought it would be fitting to have you two meet on your anniversary."

There was a long moment of silence on the other end of the line. Almost too long. Maybe Elizabeth's idea was backfiring.

"Mom?" he said, getting a little concerned. "Are you still there? Did you hear what I just said—?"

"Yes," his mother replied in a hushed voice that began to swell even as she uttered the single word. "Yes, I did," she repeated, and he could hear the utter joy vibrating in her voice. "Jared, does this mean what I think it does? That you've finally decided to settle down and—"

He knew that was what the message he'd just recited had implied, but he couldn't let her continue on like this, getting excited when there wasn't anything to really get excited about.

Still, if he admitted to resorting to clever lies, he'd lose his advantage and wind up having to come clean—about everything.

Megan would kill him.

So he resorted to vague nonstatements. "You'll just have to wait to find out, Mom. Unless, of course, you're going to San Diego, and then you'll have to wait longer for that introduction—"

"Oh, forget San Diego." He could visualize his mother waving away the whole concept of a second-honeymoon getaway. Apparently that wasn't nearly as important as what she was anticipating hearing from him. "We can always go to San Diego now that your father's retired."

He suppressed the sigh of relief that instantly rose in his chest. If his conscience bothered him a little about misleading his mother this way, he just pushed that aside.

"Then you'll let us take you out on your anniversary?" With his mother, he needed to have every *t* crossed, every *i* dotted.

"Absolutely. And Jared—" she just couldn't resist asking "—by 'us' do you mean—"

If his mother was in the same room, he would have embraced her and sent her on her way long before she got to this part.

"No more questions, Mom," he told her gently. "You'll just have to wait. All I can tell you is that we have a surprise for you."

"I can't wait," she told him, her voice bubbling with anticipation. After a few more brief words, his mother ended the conversation.

"I take it that your parents aren't going away?" Elizabeth asked as he put his phone away.

"No, they're not." Thanks to her, he thought. Elizabeth was pretty good in a mini crisis. A very handy woman to have around, he couldn't help thinking. "That was really quick thinking on your part," he told her. "Thanks."

She nodded. "No problem." Then, looking a tad closer at him, she said, "I can't help but notice that for someone whose plan is back on track, you don't look very happy."

He didn't like lying. Even for a good cause like this one. Lies had a way of coming back and blowing up in your face.

"I'm just hoping that the surprise party—and seeing all their friends and family gathered together—is enough to make her forget that she's expecting me to produce a significant other for her perusal."

"You never told her that," Elizabeth reminded him.

"But nevertheless, that's what she's thinking," he countered.

She thought of her father. He was low-key about it, but she knew he wanted to see her with someone—a soulmate who would be there for her through everything. He didn't know that the epic romance that he was hoping would bring her true happiness was the very thing that filled her with fear. She didn't believe that it was better to have loved and lost the way he did. Not when losing was so horribly painful.

"All parents think like that," she told Jared. "They want to see their kids settled into a relationship—especially if they have a good one of their own," she added. "From what I gather, your parents are incredibly compatible and happy together."

He and Megan were lucky that way, he thought. They had two parents who never even raised their voices in anger to each other. While he was growing up, a lot of his friends had parents who had split up for one reason or another and sometimes homes were turned into verbal battlefields. His friends all liked to come to his house because the love there just seem to radiate outward, touching each and every person who walked in through the door.

"They are," he said proudly. And then he recalled that she'd mentioned losing her mother at an early age. He wondered if she thought he was bragging. "Sorry," he murmured, "I didn't mean to sound insensitive."

Where had that come from? she wondered. "You weren't. And as for worrying about your mom being disappointed, just tell her that you were desperate not to spoil the surprise and that the idea about introducing her to someone special on the big day was mine." She flashed a grin at him. "I'll take the fall, no extra charge."

He laughed then, all the tension that had been there just a moment ago completely dissipating. He looked at her appreciatively. "You really are something else, you know?"

"So my brothers keep telling me, except that their tone when they say it is usually somewhat accusatory." For just a second, she didn't try to pretend that her pulse wasn't racing madly because he was looking at her in a way that threatened to melt her right where she stood. She savored it instead. "I like the way you say it much better."

"I'll keep that in mind," he promised. "So," he continued, getting down to business, "I think everything is set for the big day. The reception hall is reserved for the night, the menu's been arranged, the RSVPs have all come in and the music has been selected." Smiling in satisfaction, he rested his eyes on Elizabeth and was pleased to see the look of approval on her face.

"And, the most important part, your parents' attendance has just been confirmed," she added whimsically.

He inclined his head. "My parents have been confirmed," he echoed, "thanks again to you." He took a deep breath. "Looks like everything's all in place."

He was stalling and he knew it. There was an elephant in the room and he needed to address it rather than just circle it. Otherwise, who knew what was actually going on in Elizabeth's head as a result of what had happened before his mother's untimely call? The lovely violinist struck him as being too polite to read him the riot act, even if his attention had been unwanted.

And yet, he had this feeling deep down in his gut that the woman who had been on the other end of that passionate kiss wasn't exactly a pushover.

Still, he needed to apologize—just in case. "Um, Elizabeth?"

She didn't like the sound of that, she thought, but she managed to keep her thoughts from registering on her face. "Yes?"

Why was it that he could talk reluctant clients into launching extensive ad campaigns yet have his brain turn into a single-cell amoeba when it came to talking to Elizabeth?

"About before…"

"When before?" she asked innocently.

"Before my mother's call."

She turned her face up to his, the picture of dewy innocence. A dewy innocent who was capable of returning his fiery kisses.

"Yes?"

He felt as if he were physically pushing each word out of his mouth. "If I was out of line—"

She raised her eyes to his. He wasn't trying to back away, he was apologizing, she realized. Time to put him out of his obvious misery.

"Did I give you that impression? That I thought you were being out of line?"

"No," he admitted. That wasn't the impression he'd gotten at all; however, there might have been a reason for that. "But you could have just been polite—"

His answer caught her off guard. And suggested something she hadn't thought of before. "Was I that boring?" she wanted to know.

"What?" How had he given her that impression? She was anything *but.* "No," he told her with a great deal of feeling. "I just didn't want you to think that was part of our…"

What word did he use here? *Arrangement? Deal?* Nothing seemed to aptly fit. And why the hell did this feel so awkward?

Maybe it's because she matters, a voice somewhere deep in his mind whispered in his head.

"Arrangement," he finally settled on for lack of a proper way to express his thoughts. "I don't want you to feel obligated to let me kiss you."

She had thought that men like this had faded away in the last century, pressed between the pages of a classic romance. Obviously, there was one modern-day counterpart left.

"Let's get something straight here," she told him in a no-nonsense voice. "I did not 'let' you kiss me. The way

I saw it, we kissed each other. And," she added, emotionally taking a step back, "at least one of us liked it."

"One of us?" he asked a little uncertainly.

Was he being coy, or telling her something? This male-female thing was a lot harder than it looked, she decided.

"Well," she began slowly, feeling her way around the conversation, "since I'm not a mind reader, I can only speak for myself. Whether or not you liked it is something that you're going to have to decide for yourself."

He nodded. "You're right. You know what I'm going to need in order to do that?"

Humor danced along the curve of her mouth as she thought she knew what was coming. "No, what?"

"Another test run," he told her, as solemnly as a preacher speaking at a Sunday sermon.

"A test run," she echoed, laughter threatening to burst free. "Is that what you call it?"

"Actually," he said, slowly closing the distance between them, "if you must know, I call it very, very exciting."

There went her pulse again, she thought, trying to outrace the speed of sound. "Well, if you put it that way, I guess you can have another crack at it."

Jared framed her face with his hands, his eyes already caressing her. "Don't mind if I do," he whispered, his voice low and husky, as he brought his mouth down to hers.

This time, it felt as if heaven and earth exploded at the very same time, creating a brave new world just large enough to accommodate the two of them.

And this time, the kiss lasted a little longer, lit a fire that burned a little brighter as well as a good deal hotter.

And just when it seemed as if they were the only two people left in the world, the sound of a ringing phone once again harshly intruded into paradise, shattering their perfect moment.

Elizabeth pulled back first, startled this time. Jared leaned his forehead against hers. He sighed and she almost laughed at the definite feeling of déjà vu.

Her sigh echoed his. That kiss had taken her to the brink of forever, and now it was gone.

So near and yet, so far.

"I'm beginning to think that the forces of nature are against us," she confessed.

His sentiments exactly, now that she had put them into words. "Yeah. Me too," Jared agreed.

Chapter Twelve

This time, however, the phone that was ringing so very intrusively belonged to Elizabeth. There was no mistaking the sound. The call was coming in on her landline.

By the time Elizabeth crossed the room and managed to reach her telephone, the answering machine had picked up. She was about to shrug and let the caller leave a message if they were so inclined.

However, when she heard the deep baritone voice and the measured cadence asking, "Are you there, Elizabeth?" she made a grab for the receiver, aborting any further message from being recorded.

She'd know that voice anywhere.

"Dad?"

"Elizabeth, then you *are* home." The relief in his voice was audible.

"Yes, I— Oh God, are you at the restaurant?" she asked, suddenly remembering that today was Thursday and unless she was working, she and her father had a standing date for dinner on Thursdays at her favorite restaurant, The Manor on the Hill.

"As a matter of fact, I am. The waiters are beginning to drift by my table, looking at me with pitying glances," her father told her, only partially kidding.

"Oh, Dad, I'm so sorry. Something came up at the last minute," she told him evasively, avoiding looking in Jared's direction. "And I didn't realize what time it was...."

"Or what day, apparently," her father surmised. "So, this 'something,' does he have a name?" he asked her good-naturedly.

The question caught her completely off guard. "How did you know? I mean—"

Stumped, Elizabeth had no idea where to go from here. She wasn't the kind who played word games with people, especially not with her father. She never had been. She had always been completely honest with the people in her life. It was one of the reasons that her father not only trusted her implicitly but also treated her as if she were an adult long before she had chronologically reached that plateau.

Trapped, Elizabeth sighed. She had no choice but to come clean. If nothing else, lies required far too complicated measures to keep them up.

"How *did* you know?" she asked.

"Elementary, my dear Elizabeth." He chuckled knowingly. "If it was a job that was keeping you away from our standing Thursday night date, you would have already called me earlier in the week, all excited about it."

He had been extremely supportive of her chosen

vocation, despite the fact that he felt that being a musician all but guaranteed lifelong poverty for all but the fortunate few. He was supportive because he knew that playing the violin made her incredibly happy and, above all, he wanted her to be happy. Luckily, he knew he was in a position to help her out financially if it ever came to that. So far, it hadn't. She was managing rather well and he was very proud of her. Just as he knew that Annie would have been, were she still alive.

Her curiosity aroused, she deliberately turned her back to Jared and lowered her voice before asking her father, "And I wouldn't have been excited if I'd met someone?"

"You, my darling daughter, are very, very cautious when it comes to letting people in." In that, he had to admit, she took after him. It had taken him six months to admit to himself that he was head over heels in love with Annie. And after she'd died, he'd shut himself off from that avenue completely.

"Really?" she countered defensively. "Someone told me just the other week that I was the friendliest person they knew."

"And I'm sure he or she thought they were right. Because they were dealing with your public persona. But the Elizabeth who exists within is exceptionally careful when it comes to her personal life. And that is probably my fault," he admitted with a heavy heart.

He'd kept her much too close much too long, enjoying her company. His daughter had been far more mature than her age warranted and there were times when he actually forgot that she was still a child. He always talked to her as if she was already an adult and she'd responded to that, but maybe he shouldn't have gone that route with her. Maybe he should have forced her to interact more with people her own age. Maybe she would have been more open that way, more receptive to forging a relationship.

"Your fault?" she repeated, then teased, "Not possible, Dad. You don't have a fault in your entire body."

He smiled to himself, signaling for a waiter to come over and give him a check for the chardonnay he'd been sipping as he'd waited for Elizabeth to arrive.

"You're right, I forgot," he acknowledged with a soft, appreciative laugh. "So, next Thursday—provided you're free, of course."

"Next Thursday," she agreed, deliberately not commenting on whether or not she was going to be free. She knew her father assigned a far deeper meaning to that word than she did. "And to make this up to you, it'll be my treat."

"I won't argue with that, but you have nothing to make up for," he informed her. "It's not as if we were on the trapeze, with you being my catcher and suddenly disappearing on me. Remember, Elizabeth, this is the time to really enjoy yourself," he reminded her. "When you're young."

She knew it would do her no good to argue the point, or to insist that his assumption in this case was baseless. He wasn't about to be convinced. Her protests would just have the reverse effect.

And besides, she didn't want to keep Jared waiting much longer.

"I love you, Dad," she said, ending the call the way she usually did.

"And I you," her father replied.

Hanging up, John gave it to the count of five to make certain the connection was terminated and then he hit a series of numbers, making another call. There were things he wanted to ask Maizie Sommers—not to mention give her his colossal thanks.

"That was my dad," Elizabeth told Jared, putting the receiver back into its cradle.

"I had my suspicions," Jared deadpanned. And then, his mouth quirking into a smile, he added, "Hearing you say 'Dad' when you picked up the phone kind of gave it away." He paused for a second, debating asking the next question, then decided that honesty was the best policy. "You stood him up?"

"Not intentionally," she protested, then decided to face up to her failing. "But yes, I guess I did."

"How long have you been doing it?" he wanted to know. Then, in case she misunderstood, Jared clarified his question by adding, "Having dinner with your dad on Thursdays?"

Her smile was wrapped in fond memories. "Ever since college. I didn't go away even though I was supposed to—I was accepted by a college back East—and to keep abreast of my life, he started this little tradition where he would take me out to dinner, and we'd talk about what was going on in each of our lives," she volunteered. "I have to admit that I looked forward to it just as much as he did," she told him. "Maybe even more. It gave me a sense of being connected."

And that, Jared gathered, was very important to her. He could relate to that. "Is he angry?" he asked.

She shook her head. "My dad doesn't get angry—No, I take that back," she amended. "I did see my father get angry just once. When my mother died, he got angry at God."

Jared released a low, appreciative whistle. "Boy, your father doesn't fool around, does he? Goes right for the big target, no small-time stuff for him," he said wryly.

"Other than that one time, my dad has always been the gentlest, kindest man I know. I never had a time when I felt he was cramping my style, or being critical of any of my choices. He's always been there for me, always been nothing but supportive—of my brothers as well as me," she added in case she'd made it sound as if her father played favorites.

He nodded. "I know what you mean. I kind of feel the same way about my father. About both my parents," he amended. "While a lot of my friends in school had parents who split up, mine seemed to have something very special going on. Something rare," he underscored. "So rare that the average relationship just wouldn't measure up. I always felt that if I couldn't have that, I didn't want anything."

It was, he reminded himself, one of the reasons he'd never even thought about settling down himself. Because he had this shining example of happiness before him and knew that he didn't want to settle for anything less.

At the same time, he knew how much less there could be out there. He'd heard his friends' horror stories, been there for some while their parents were in the throes of divorces that seemed as if they were forged in hell. That was something he knew he would have wanted to avoid at all cost.

He felt that if he couldn't have a relationship that was as perfect as the union that his parents had, then he didn't want anything at all.

Besides, this was the twenty-first century. Not getting married, not having a family, those choices were acceptable now. No one looked at you as if there were something wrong with you. Remaining single for the rest of your life was just as normal as being married. It was all about choices.

Or, conversely, it was about *not* making choices. About abstaining from making any life-altering decisions—ever.

But now he was beginning to think that maybe what his parents had wasn't so incredibly unique and unattainable after all. Maybe it just took having someone unique come into his life. Making him think…

Making him wonder what if…?

"I think my father felt that way about my mother," Elizabeth was saying. "That she was one in a million. After she died, he had a very hard time coming to grips with everything, but then he finally rallied. Because of us—his kids," she explained.

She could remember it as if it were all just yesterday, instead of more than two decades ago. "My maternal grandmother offered to take us in, saying that men had a hard time raising children on their own and that since my dad was a doctor, he wouldn't be around much anyway. She'd spare him the guilt that neglect generated by taking us with her back to Georgia and raising us." A fond smile curved her lips as she relived that period.

"That was when he came out of the tailspin he was in. I was only five, but I remember the look on his face when he realized my grandmother was telling him he could just walk away from us. He had this very strange look in his eyes and right then and there, he boxed up all the pain that was tearing him apart and pushed it into some faraway compartment in his mind. And just like that—" she snapped her fingers "—he was himself again. He was my dad.

"He told my grandmother in a very quiet voice that he was our father and that we belonged with him. He said nothing in the world was going to change that. My grandmother flew back to Georgia the very next morning. Alone."

As she paused, her revelation taking a momentary toll on her, Elizabeth realized that somehow she'd wound up monopolizing the conversation.

"How did we wind up talking about that?" she asked, suddenly feeling embarrassed.

"We were trading notes on parents," he reminded her, then steered the conversation into neutral waters. "I guess it's safe to say that we're both pretty lucky. Some of my friends had parents they had to make an appointment with just to see them when they were growing up." He saw Elizabeth looking at him skeptically and he relented somewhat. "Okay, maybe I'm exaggerating," he admitted. "But not by much."

He was even luckier to have both parents still alive, she couldn't help thinking. "I can see why giving them this surprise celebration is so important to you," she told him.

The anniversary celebration made him remember the

length he had to go to in order to ensure that his parents would be there to receive their well-earned congratulations from family and friends.

"I'm just hoping my mother likes it enough to forgive me for lying to her."

He really looked concerned, she realized. That put him, quite possibly, in a class by himself. Not many men worried about the effects of a lie they'd told.

She decided to change his stand on that. "That wasn't a lie."

"Oh? Then what would you have called it?"

That was easy enough to answer. "A desperate measure undertaken for your mom's own good. You didn't want to have to resort to spoiling the surprise for her," she said, "so you really had no choice in the matter. You had to tell her *something* to keep her and your father in town for the party, and promising to introduce her to someone she believes is important in your life did the trick."

His parents taking off instead of turning up at their own surprise party had greater repercussions than just that. "Not to mention that Megan would read me the riot act if she found out I told them about the party to keep them in town. She'd probably go into premature labor right there just to get back at me."

Elizabeth grinned. She had no idea he was capable of that level of exaggeration. "Well, if nothing else, that would take care of the entertainment portion of your evening," she teased.

He could just see that—on second thought, he most definitely did *not* want to see that. "I don't think Megan would exactly see it your way. She hates feeling like a walrus, which is the way she describes herself these days. The only thing she hates more than that is the thought of the pain she's in for when she eventually goes into labor."

"Labor doesn't necessarily have to be bad," she told Jared. "I've heard stories that some women actually have had an easy time of it."

He laughed shortly, shaking his head. "Megan has *never* had an easy time of it—no matter what's involved." His sister had a tendency to overdramatize everything. She was the type that if she sneezed, she was convinced she was coming down with a fatal strain of pneumonia. "It's not in her nature. Her kid will probably be in therapy by the time he or she is three months old."

That didn't sound very promising, she thought. "Maybe your sister'll change once the baby is born. Babies have a way of doing that."

"I hope you're right—for her husband's sake as well as the baby's," he said, although he had to admit he had his doubts. Megan, unfortunately, wasn't anything like Elizabeth.

The moment the thought occurred to him, he looked at Elizabeth thoughtfully. He really liked the upbeat way she viewed things. "Are you always this optimistic?"

Elizabeth lifted and then lowered her shoulders in a vague shrug.

"I do my best. Being a pessimist brings not only the person having dark thoughts down, but it brings down everyone around that person as well. Personally, I like leaving people with a smile, not depressing thoughts." That had always been her goal, ever since she'd first succeeded in making her father smile by playing her mother's violin. "That's why I love the violin," she explained.

He couldn't see the connection. "Come again?"

"Depending on what you play," she told him, "you can either bring tears to someone's eyes or a smile to their lips."

"And you can do that with a violin?" he asked, somewhat skeptical of the claim.

"Absolutely. I can give you a demonstration if you like," she offered.

He had no doubt that she could back up her claim. She was a remarkable woman who, he was growing to believe, could do anything she set her mind to. But right now, he wasn't all that interested in listening to a private concert. He was more interested in regaining the foothold that had been established before his mother and her father had interrupted.

"I know another way to bring about that smile you mentioned."

Was it just her, or was that incredibly seductive-sounding?

There went her heart again, beating like a drummer working his way to a crescendo. She barely had enough oxygen to utter, "Oh?"

"Yes. If you'd like, I could give *you* a demonstration," he offered, turning her words back around to her.

Her lips were all but stuck together. She nodded, then managed to whisper almost haltingly, "All right." Elizabeth found herself out of breath by the second word.

Jared's eyes held hers prisoner as he slowly slipped his arms around her.

But just before he lowered his mouth to hers, he stopped.

Her breath caught in her throat.

Was something wrong?

Had he decided he was getting too involved with someone he'd hired, someone who, however temporarily, was employed by him?

Elizabeth debated just drawing back, or possibly saying something flippant and face-saving—although for the life of her, she didn't know what—when she saw Jared taking his phone out.

Was he going to call someone?

Now?

But rather than placing a call, he turned the phone off.

"This time, no interruptions," he told her, placing the phone on the coffee table.

Incredibly relieved and just as equally charged with anticipation, Elizabeth did the same with her phone.

"No interruptions," she echoed.

And there weren't any.

Chapter Thirteen

He hadn't planned this.

But he would have been lying if he pretended that he hadn't thought about it.

He had.

More than once.

Thought about what it might be like to explore Elizabeth's soft, stirring body. To slowly peel away her clothing and discover if what he'd envisioned when his imagination had taken flight was actually better than the real thing.

Or if, just possibly, fantasy ultimately didn't hold a candle to reality.

But in every version, whether in the one where he stopped on the threshold of discovery, or in the one where the exploratory venture was taken all the way to completion, sanity and clearheadedness had always managed to prevail.

But not so in reality.

Because he found himself utterly breathless almost from the first moment, breathless and eager, as something that he'd grown rather accustomed to enjoying morphed into an entirely new experience for him.

For him, anticipation had always been the best part of lovemaking because once the ground was tread and the walls breached, the experience was no more unique than the last one had been.

But this, this just kept building rather than ebbing. This was a bouquet of surprises that he couldn't even begin to accurately anticipate. And even if he could, anticipation simply could not compare to what was happening.

At first, he'd only meant to kiss Elizabeth.

And then, he told himself, he only wanted to kiss her a little more, a little longer, perhaps a little more passionately.

But that road didn't lead to a jumping-off place. It only led deeper into the forest of desires.

It was a simple matter of the more he kissed her, the more he *wanted* to kiss her.

The more he wanted.

In a confused attempt to stem the rising tide of passion, he held her to him, fitting her body against his. But the moment he did, he realized his mistake. Because doing that just led to something more.

Led to a greater yearning.

Jared didn't remember trailing his hands along the sides of her body, absorbing the delicate swell of her breasts, but the moment he did so, the flame within him flared like a backdraft, threatening to set him on fire.

But hard though it was, he would have refrained from filling his hands with her supple flesh. He would have left her clothes in place and struggled mightily to finally break the connection, to back away. He would have—had she not begun to tug on his shirt, separating the buttons from their holes and dragging the material off his shoulders.

That spelled his complete undoing.

He felt his stomach muscles contracting, felt the rest of him all but dissolving as the raw need to touch her, to make love with her, threatened to utterly consume him.

After that, everything seemed to become a hazy frenzy.

Jared vaguely remembered leading her to the couch and helping her tug away his clothing. Remembered more acutely removing hers as his fingers interfered with hers, his eagerness feeding hers and hers his, creating a swirling cauldron of heat, desire and the promise of ultimate fulfillment that shimmered on the horizon.

She had no idea what came over her. No idea how one thing just kept leading to another and then another. Instead, she discovered what it meant to be on the brink of losing her ability to think, to be rational, to act on her better instincts.

The instincts she was aware of now all focused on sustaining this wondrous pleasure she was experiencing, on simultaneously receiving it and giving it.

Everywhere his lips touched, she could feel her anticipation heightening, could feel her eagerness multiplying, so that it seemed to totally consume her in ways she'd never imagined.

It was in the very air she breathed.

She'd always been so rational before, enjoying the few times that she'd found herself at this point, in this position, making love with someone.

But during all those times, her mind had never taken a hiatus. She'd never just focused on her reaction, on attaining that delicious explosion and coaxing one from her partner as well.

This time, though, it was different.

Everything with Jared was different, she realized before she was incapable of connecting her thoughts anymore.

And then, just like that, she didn't care about anything.

Didn't care that she wanted to keep a tight rein on herself because to fully give of herself was to leave herself completely vulnerable and that had always filled her with fear.

Moreover, she didn't remember to compartmentalize her feelings so that her sense of self-preservation wasn't lost. All that had been born of apprehension. Fear of abandonment, of being left behind, to cope and to carry on no matter how much pain her heart was in.

And while she envied what her parents had had, she never wanted to leave herself open to the utter heartache that loving someone so completely, with all her heart, ushered in.

Elizabeth didn't want to follow in her father's footsteps.

But all those well-thought-out safeguards that were supposed to protect her heart had gotten lost somehow, burned to a crisp in the fires of this incredible longing that Jared had created within her.

Created just by kissing her.

Fed just by touching her.

As his lips trailed along her skin, causing her to twist and turn into him, Elizabeth did what she could to hold on to that last bit of control and keep it from slipping away.

It was an effort doomed to failure.

The very next moment, she felt herself being swept away, arching her back so as to somehow absorb the sensation even more thoroughly than she had. At the same time, the acute ache, the sweet agony of the climax he'd generated, was almost too much for her to contain.

Elizabeth cried out his name, grasping at him, pulling him back toward her.

He'd forged a path of heat along her bare skin, beginning at her forehead and ending at the most sensitive part of her, at her very core.

Pulling himself up again so that their faces were level, his arms bracketing her upper torso, Jared knew he hadn't the strength to hold back any longer. Even if he wanted to draw out the moment one second longer, he couldn't.

With his heart pounding harder than he recalled it ever doing, Jared lowered his hips to hers, driving himself into her slowly with the last shred of restraint he had.

And then the last band of self-control was ruptured.

The tempo, begun whisper slow, built, increasing almost recklessly.

He felt her grasp on to his shoulders, felt her matching his movements, driven by the same frantic melody that was playing over and over in his head.

And then he was there.

And she was with him.

He didn't need to ask, to guess, he knew. The pinnacle was reached simultaneously by both of them and, suddenly, they were airborne, diving off the edge while holding hands.

Free-falling to earth together.

Ever so slowly, the euphoria tiptoed back, receding, taking the multicolored beams of the dazzling rainbow with it. Uncovering the world that it had temporarily hidden beneath its rays.

He'd never been good at small talk, especially not in a situation that could easily have become very uncomfortable.

The words that rose to his lips hadn't been filtered through his brain first, hadn't come from some well-thumbed afterglow handbook. They just seemed to emerge of their own accord.

"That was incredible," he murmured, punctuating his statement with a kiss that he pressed to her forehead.

Her forehead was damp, he noted. Just like the rest of him was.

That was incredible.

Did he say that to all the women he made love with? she wondered.

Part of her almost wished that he did and that she would somehow be able to prove it for sure. Because if he did, if he was callous enough to use the same lines on different women, well, that would remove him from

her heart—a place where he seemed to be firmly em-
bedded.

Oh God, she couldn't let him stay there. She just
couldn't. She couldn't let herself feel this way about
him.

But what is the harm? a little voice in her head whispered. *Just for a little while, what is the harm? Enjoy
it, enjoy yourself, and then move on. You'll be okay if
you know it won't last.*

But would she? Would she be okay? And, more to
the point, would she be able to get herself to move on?

She was afraid that she knew the answer to both of
those questions.

"I don't know about you," Jared continued after several beats had gone by. "But I may never move again.
I've never felt so exhausted in my life," he confessed.
His words were accompanied by a mighty sigh that
seemed to come from his very toes.

She raised her head and then drew her elbow against
her, propping herself up on the couch for a second to
look at him. And then she splayed her hands along his
broad chest and rested her head there.

"Completely exhausted?" she asked in a voice that
sounded far too innocent not to have something hidden
just beneath the surface.

"Yes." It took effort to form even that word.

Very slowly, she drew herself up along his body until
their torsos were strategically level. "You're sure you're
completely exhausted?"

"I'm sure— Oh, the hell with it," Jared muttered,
framing her face with his hands and drawing her mouth
down to his as he surrendered.

The moment he did, it became evident to both of them that perhaps he wasn't really as exhausted as he'd first thought.

Definitely not too tired for this, he silently amended as desire for Elizabeth, for another round of the exquisite pleasure he'd just experienced, sprang up within him, supplying him with another shot of revitalizing energy.

When Elizabeth woke up, reluctantly giving up the incredible dream she was having, it was to the sight of Jared moving around her bedroom, looking for his discarded clothing.

He was gathering up each piece as he found it, and seemed to be doing his best not to wake her.

He looked like a man about to flee, Elizabeth thought as her brain started slowly processing what she was seeing.

"Where are you going?" she asked sleepily.

Sitting up in bed, the scene of their final exquisite coupling, Elizabeth scrubbed her hands over her face in an attempt to wipe away the last of the haze from her brain so that she could grasp some semblance of clarity.

Jared froze at the sound of her voice and looked over his shoulder in her direction. He flashed an apologetic smile. "I'm sorry, I didn't want to wake you."

"Sorry. Your perfect getaway isn't so perfect I guess," she murmured.

"Getaway?" he repeated, giving her a confused look. "I'm not executing a getaway," he protested, wondering why she would even think that. "I'm just late for work."

The moment he said that, things began falling into place in her brain.

And a little bit of hope sprang up in her heart.

He *wasn't* leaving because he considered this a one-night stand.

"Oh, right. It's not the weekend yet." Buoyed by the fact that he wasn't trying to disappear, she sat up and swung her legs out of bed. "I'll make you breakfast," she volunteered.

Amused, he quirked a brow. "I thought you didn't cook."

"Toaster pastry," she enlightened him, letting him know what his breakfast was going to consist of. "I can use a toaster with the best of them."

The sheet had pooled around her hips, affording him an enticing view that, despite the fact that he'd already been privy to it for the better part of the night before, still managed to make his knees completely weak. Another sign that what had happened last night wasn't something he'd just conjured up in his imagination.

This one had gotten to him.

Big-time.

"I'm afraid I'll have to sample your toaster skills some other time," he told her, stooping to pick up his shoes.

She remained sitting exactly where she was. *As* she was.

"Care to sample anything else?" she offered, her eyes meeting his, her meaning blatantly cleared.

It was on the tip of his tongue to tell her that he was an integral part of a presentation taking place this afternoon, and that he needed to toil away in the office all morning to prepare for it.

On the tip of his tongue to tell her that he couldn't afford to slack off, to indulge his more physical needs in lieu of living up to his professional responsibilities.

But none of that managed to find its way *off* the tip of his tongue and out of his mouth.

He let go of the shoes he'd just picked up, released the clothes clustered in his arms against his chest.

"Oh, the hell with it," he said for the second time in less than a day, both times announcing his utter surrender to her very potent charms. "I'll tell them I was sick this morning."

"Sick? Is that what you call it?" she asked, laughter bubbling in her throat as Jared climbed back into bed and pulled her to him.

"Incapacitated, how's that?" he asked. "Better?"

"Incapacitated," she repeated after a beat as if testing it to see how the word sounded.

Her eyes were already fluttering shut and she felt her body heating in response to the warm lips that were pressed against her neck and creating a searing trail along her skin.

"Incapacitated works for me," she pronounced, shifting her body so that she could drape her arms around his neck.

The next moment, he was lowering her back onto the mattress again, his mind cleared of everything except for his need for her.

"As long as you're okay with it," he murmured against her skin.

Elizabeth twisted so that her body was snug beneath

his, drawing his heat, creating heat of her own as she already began anticipating the fiery climax between them.

"Oh, so much more than okay," she whispered huskily before the need for words disappeared completely.

Chapter Fourteen

When she heard the chimes alerting her that someone was entering her real estate office, Maizie Sommers looked up from the notes she was writing at her desk.

Officially, the office was supposed to be closed by now. She'd already sent her people home but, as always, there were a few last-minute loose ends she wanted to tie up before she locked up for the night.

It was against her nature to send a potential client away, but at this point, she was tired and nursing the hope that whoever had just set the chimes off had wandered into her office by mistake.

And then she saw who it was and knew it was no mistake.

John Stephens crossed to her desk and presented her with a very large, very fragrant bouquet of perfect yellow roses.

The warm smile on her lips was somewhat bemused. "Flowers?"

Maizie placed the bouquet on her desk and went to the golden oak cabinets that lined one back wall. Opening the section to the extreme right, she took out the cut-glass vase that had been her late husband's last anniversary gift to her.

Filling the vase with tap water, she returned to her desk, and John.

"I know you too well to think you've suddenly decided to go courting and thought you'd brush up your technique on a willing subject." Removing the green tissue paper from the stems, she arranged the roses one by one in the vase, taking care that none of the flowers was crowded. "So, tell me," she coaxed. "Why are you bringing me roses?"

"To thank you for a job well done," he told her simply.

Maizie's eyebrows drew together as traces of confusion registered on her face. "I'm afraid that I don't—" And then a smile lit up her face as it hit her. "You're talking about Elizabeth, aren't you?"

"I am." John's own smile widened as he filled her in. "Elizabeth forgot about our standing Thursday dinner."

"She stood you up?" Maizie asked in surprise. That definitely didn't sound like something that his daughter would do. But rather than feel slighted, he seemed exceptionally happy about it. Maizie went back to being befuddled. Was this about the match she had helped put into motion, or—?

John inclined his head. "She did."

Maizie continued to try to piece things together. "And you're happy about that?"

"Absolutely." And then he gave her the last crucial piece of information. "There was someone with her when I called to make sure she was all right. It was obvious that this 'someone' had made her lose track of everything else, including what day of the week it was." He smiled at Maizie. "And I have you to thank for that."

So, it *was* about the match. Still, she didn't believe in counting chickens until they had fully abandoned their shells.

"Well, don't thank me yet," Maizie cautioned. She didn't want the man to get ahead of himself just yet, even though, so far, each match that she, Theresa and Cecilia had put together were all going strong. "And, when the time does come for thanks, you actually have Theresa to thank for this," she informed him. "I personally haven't seen the young man in question, but Theresa vouched for him and she has excellent radar."

"Does she now?" John asked jovially.

"Affirmative. She told me that Jared was a repeat customer who'd used her catering company several times. This particular time he's having her cater his parents' thirty-fifth anniversary celebration—he's planning to surprise them. In my book, that makes him a wonderful young man." She saw her friend's smile grow a little forced around the edges. Her mother's radar was instantly alerted. "Is something wrong, John?"

He shook his head. "No, everything's fine," he told her perhaps a bit too emphatically. "Just fine," he repeated.

"You know you're quite possibly getting what you wished for," she pointed out.

There was an unexpected melancholy feeling that had materialized out of nowhere and threatened to hover over him. He wasn't supposed to feel this way, he told himself. "Yes, I know."

Maizie looked at him knowingly. She knew *exactly* what he was feeling. "But nonetheless, it is a little hard to accept, now that it's happening, isn't it?"

John looked at her, somewhat startled at how close to home her comment had hit. He wanted to deny her assumption—but that would be lying. "When did you get to be so wise, Maizie?"

Maizie laughed. That was easy enough to answer. "When I started dabbling in matchmaking to set up my own daughter. Theresa, Cecilia and I made a pact that we wouldn't stop until we had all four of our children in committed relationships."

He thought a moment. "As I recall, all of them are married now."

"Yes, they are," she told him proudly. "And, I don't mind telling you, success is a little bittersweet because marriage, more than anything else, makes you realize just how grown up your child actually is." And then she flashed him a bright, understanding smile. "But it *is* the right thing to root for," she assured him.

"I know." And he did, even though in his heart of hearts, he felt that no man would ever be quite good enough for his little girl.

With her computer powered down, there was nothing left for Maizie to do but turn out the lights and lock up. "You know, it's been rather a hectic day. I need to wind down a little bit. Why don't I lock up and buy you dinner to celebrate this possible success?" she suggested.

"You don't have to do that, Maizie," he protested.

"I know. But I'd like to. It'll give me a chance to show you some baby pictures I've just transferred to my phone. It's a lot easier if I have a captive audience," she told him with a wink.

John laughed as he rose from the chair and followed her to the front door. "I think I'd like that," he admitted.

Maizie's eyes sparkled. "Good, because you really didn't have a choice in the matter, you know."

Elizabeth kept pushing the thought from her mind, but she knew that what she was doing was tantamount to treading on thin ice. The evening of the anniversary celebration was swiftly approaching, and with it, more than likely, the end of the exquisite interlude she was caught up in.

All along she'd known that this had a limited life span—whatever "this" actually was, she thought with a heartfelt sigh.

Right now, under one pretext or another, she and Jared were still getting together every evening, either at her apartment or his place of work. Or twice, he'd met her at the banquet hall. When they'd met there, it revolved around making final decisions on seating, decorations and flowers at the celebration. Because Megan was still away on the cruise, Jared told her he felt he needed a woman to help him with the various selections. He tactfully refrained from mentioning that Megan called him regularly.

"What do I know about decorations?" he'd asked

with an exaggerated shrug when she'd asked him what motif he was going with at the party. "I don't even have a Christmas tree up in December."

She'd met his words with a laugh, then stopped dead when she realized that he was actually serious.

"You're not kidding, are you?" Elizabeth had asked, stunned.

When he shook his head, confirming her suspicions, her first impulse was to say that she could remedy that for him, just as she had for her brothers when they'd each struck out on their own and moved into their first bachelor apartments.

But she knew that was presuming way too much. Christmas was more than six months away. She sincerely doubted Jared would even remember her name in six months, much less that she'd promised to rekindle his waning holiday spirit by getting him to put up a traditional Christmas tree.

And she was okay with that, Elizabeth convinced herself. Because she expected that, even planned for that, since the flip side of that scenario would be one in which they were together—and she would be silently waiting for the shoe to fall and the gut-wrenching emptiness to descend on her with piercing precision.

Walking away on her own terms, at a time of her choosing, was a far better way to go because it meant that she was in control of her own life.

Or so she kept telling herself.

"No, I'm not kidding," Jared was saying, oblivious to the internal war she was waging right in front of him. "Why?" he asked. "Are you offering to civilize me? Turn me into a Christmas decoration junkie?"

"Only if you want me to," she heard herself saying rather than the single resounding "no" she'd geared herself up to deliver.

"Okay," Jared agreed, nodding, thinking that it might really be fun to have someone to decorate a tree with. And *everything* seemed to be more fun with her around to share it with. "But first I need help wading through all this." He pointed to a stack of photographs, all depicting different centerpieces of the tables at the reception. "What do you think of this one?"

"Too cute," she pronounced. Flashing him a smile, she got down to business and eventually narrowed down his choices to a very manageable two.

The moment she placed the two photographs in front of him, Jared saw that they were really the only two viable contenders. She'd managed to home in on the best of the best, he realized in awe.

Elizabeth was a godsend, he couldn't help thinking, in more ways than one.

Who knew, he speculated. Maybe by the time that the night of the party came around, when he introduced her to his parents, Elizabeth would be more than just a key player in the musical ensemble he'd hired for the celebration.

Maybe she'd wind up being exactly what he'd initially pretended she would be for his mother's benefit.

The thought was definitely not without merit, he caught himself thinking.

The evening went the same way all their evenings had gone. After each pretense for the get-together was handled, he'd suggest that they get something to eat.

That in turn would always lead to them winding up

the night in her apartment—or in his, no longer talking about the event that had brought her into his life. They'd become far too busy with more pleasurable pursuits.

The first time he'd brought her over to his place, she'd made a mental note to call Amanda as soon as she could to tell her friend that her suspicions that Jared might be married were not just completely baseless, but dead wrong.

His apartment was somewhat neater than the abodes her own brothers inhabited, but it definitely had that man-on-his-own state of chaos about it.

The first time she'd been invited over, Elizabeth fought the urge to clean up for as long as she could, then, when Jared went into another room to show her the gift he was giving his parents, she surrendered.

When he walked back into the living room where he'd left her, Elizabeth had her arms filled with the newspapers he'd haphazardly pushed under the coffee table. His theory of cleaning was obviously out of sight, out of mind. She thought she could get to the trash before he came back in, but she'd miscalculated.

Putting the folder containing the anniversary gift down, Jared looked at her, somewhat bemused. "What are you doing?"

"Recycling?" she'd offered hopefully, saying the first thing that came to her mind.

Nothing a man hated more than a woman who tried to change their ways, that's what her brothers had told her. The last thing she wanted was for Jared to think she was trying to take over or settle in. She just had trouble ignoring clutter.

Crossing to her, Jared took the newspapers out of

her arms and dropped them—this time on *top* of the coffee table rather than under it.

"I didn't bring you over here because I wanted you to clean my place up," he informed her.

The very way he'd said it seemed to hold an unspoken promise. One that caused her pulse to speed up and her body temperature to rise in sheer anticipation.

Elizabeth cocked her head, her eyes locking with his. After a moment, she asked, "And exactly why did you bring me over here?"

It was a leading question, one they both knew the answer to, at least intuitively if not in so many actual words.

"Well, part of the reason was to ask your opinion on this." Picking up the folder, he opened it and produced two first-class, round-trip tickets to Paris, as well as an all-expenses-paid, two-week stay at a luxurious hotel in the City of Lights. "My parents always wanted to go there, but the timing was never right, not to mention the fact that they felt it was too expensive an indulgence."

"Well, off the top of my head, *my* opinion is that you're a really fantastic son," she told him honestly. "They are going to really *love* that." She eyed him expectantly. "And the other part?"

"Hmm?" he murmured, perhaps just a tad too innocently to be convincing.

"You said that was part of the reason you asked me here," she reminded him, then prodded, "What's the other part of the reason?"

Tucking the two tickets back into the folder and leaving them on the coffee table beside the newspapers he'd dropped, Jared proceeded to fill his arms with her. He laced his fingers together behind her back and pulled her to him.

Fitting her torso against his was now becoming a very familiar feeling that nevertheless still managed to send his batteries into overdrive.

"Why do you think?" he murmured seductively, his eyes already making love to her.

She did her best to look innocent. "How many guesses do I get?"

"None," he answered a second before his lips found hers.

Then they fell into bed as they did each and every evening.

As always, the exquisite lovemaking they enjoyed throughout the night took her breath away. But even though their interlude was mind-bogglingly wonderful, it was marred by the thought that their time together was quickly coming to an end.

But Elizabeth stubbornly shut that notion down whenever it would pop up in the back of her mind... and as the days—and nights—flew by, she suspected this worry didn't cross Jared's mind at all. She had no reason to believe that he contemplated their future because, other than the casual reference to the Christmas tree that one time, Jared hadn't mentioned life after the anniversary celebration.

The celebration was the end goal, the focal point of all their ultimate efforts.

Beyond that lay nothing. No plans, no future, no anticipated activity.

Nothing.

Elizabeth did her best to convince herself that she

was all right with that, but in all honesty, the closer the anniversary party drew, the more restless she felt inside.

Despite the fact that, ultimately, *this* was what she wanted. A wonderful time with no strings, no promises—and no danger of having her heart ripped out of her chest because it had never gotten that emotionally involved in the first place.

The hell it hasn't, that annoying little voice in her head insisted.

She did her best to block that out as well, but she was becoming less and less successful as the voice became more and more adamant.

"All right, I admit it," Megan said, her manner somewhat dejected after she had reviewed everything that her brother had taken care of in her absence. "You don't need me."

"Of course he needs you," Elizabeth assured her with feeling, jumping in.

Jared had insisted she accompany him when he presented everything for his sister's final review. He'd surprised her by saying that he needed the moral support. Although she'd only known Megan for approximately thirty-two minutes, she'd taken an instant liking to his slightly fussy younger sister.

"If you hadn't laid out all the groundwork for him," Elizabeth stressed, "Jared wouldn't have had a clue where to get started or how."

"He found you," Megan pointed out. Her inference was clear. His sister felt that she was the one who was really responsible for getting things rolling along on the right track.

But Elizabeth neatly deflected the veiled praise. "Only because he was dealing with the caterer who knew someone who, in turn, made a recommendation because they'd heard me play." She deliberately made it sound as if she had only a minor hand in all this, rather than being the one Jared had used as a sounding board. "But Jared told me you were the one who said he needed a caterer in the first place."

Not exactly relishing his role as a simpleton who needed help putting on his shoes, Jared quietly interjected, "I think I would have ultimately figured that part out."

Neither woman seemed to hear him, or, if they did, they weren't acknowledging it.

"If you hadn't left him that list, he would have been completely lost," Elizabeth concluded.

Megan looked at her in surprise. "You know about the list?"

Elizabeth did her best to suppress the smile that rose to her lips. She'd managed to pierce through Megan's dejection. "Jared showed it to me. He was impressed at how comprehensive it was," she added.

Megan perked up at the word, her confidence, for the most part, seemed to have been restored. "I guess it was pretty 'comprehensive' at that." Megan turned to look at Jared, as if suddenly realizing that he was still there. "I like her," she said, nodding toward Elizabeth.

Jared slanted a well-pleased glance in Elizabeth's direction. "Yeah. Me too."

Rather than feel triumphant at the approval and that she'd managed to make Megan feel better, all Elizabeth was aware of was that uneasiness had suddenly climbed up another notch inside her chest, even as she forced a smile to her lips.

Chapter Fifteen

"That was really quick thinking on your part," Jared said later that evening after they'd left Megan's house and had driven over to her apartment. "Not to mention kind. Megan can be a little prickly to deal with at times."

Elizabeth shrugged away the compliment, although she was rather glad he'd taken notice. "It wasn't hard to see that your sister felt unnecessary because you'd handled everything so competently. Everyone needs to be needed." To her, that was a simple fact of life she'd always found to be true. "I just made sure that your sister felt needed."

Jared laughed. "You're a pretty good diplomat," he told her, getting a kick out of her terminology. His grin widened as he echoed the phrase she'd just used. Was that her way of flattering him, or had she really meant what she'd just said? "'So competently,' huh? That was because I had you to reinforce all the weak points for me," he remarked. "And before you say anything further, I don't need to be needed—at least, not when it comes to planning events and the thousand and two things that go along with it. I do, however, like the fact that you need me."

Elizabeth felt her heart suddenly skip a beat and all her nerve endings go on high alert. She looked at him uneasily. "When did I say that?"

"You didn't have to," he told her, his lips lightly grazing hers.

Oh God, she couldn't pull together a proper defense when he was doing that. He was clouding her mind, weakening her resolve.

Making her yearn for *just one more time.*

Well, what was the harm in that? her mind silently challenged. The anniversary celebration was just two days away.

Two days, and then it would all be over. The need to get together, to see each other, to set fire to each other's worlds. All that would cease to be. Jared would go back to whatever routine he'd had before all this had begun and she, well, she would go back to doing what she seemed to do best, she thought ruefully. Providing the background music for other people's lives.

The pang that hit her with the suddenness of a speeding bullet was almost overwhelming.

So overwhelming that she became practically frenzied in her movements, in her actions. They had just barely walked across her threshold—there was leftover pizza in her refrigerator, which had provided the necessary answer to the nightly question, "Your place or mine?"—when she'd begun pulling off Jared's clothes as well as her own.

Frustration nibbled away at her because she was succeeding only marginally, sending pieces of apparel flying haphazardly about her neat-as-a-pin apartment. She thought she might have ripped off a button, or maybe torn part of his shirt, in her haste to get both of them naked as quickly as possible.

"Hey, hey, what's gotten into you?" Jared asked with a perplexed laugh as he caught both her hands in his and momentarily stilled them.

"Shut up and get your clothes off," she ordered seductively, capturing a corner of his mouth as she skimmed her lips against his.

"Yes, ma'am," he responded dutifully.

His eyes danced with humor as he shed the last of his own clothing, then covered her breasts with his hands. Absorbing the heat, he allowed it to sizzle through him for a moment.

And then he scooped her up in his arms and carried her to her bedroom, his lips urgently sealed to hers.

Using his back to push open her bedroom door all the way, he slowly crossed to the center of the room, to her bed, and gently deposited her onto it.

Their mouths momentarily separated, he found he could hardly catch his breath. He didn't know what had gotten into her, but he knew that he certainly liked the vitality, the sheer lust he'd just previewed.

"Remind me to have you talk to Megan more often," he said, only half in jest.

Then, entangling his limbs as well as his lips with

hers, he wound up dispensing with the need for any further talk for a good long while.

At times, especially when it had been in its infancy stage, Jared had begun to feel as if, like Godot, this evening he'd been planning would never come.

But it was *finally* here.

The anniversary party was under way and he had pulled it off.

They had pulled it off, he silently amended in the next breath he took. He and Megan had actually managed to surprise their parents.

To be honest, he wasn't sure just how well that would have gone had Elizabeth not agreed to play the part of his girlfriend, thereby instantly transforming into a person of immense interest, at least as far as his mother was concerned.

Adriana Winterset had been so focused on meeting the woman he supposedly considered important enough to share a major family event with that she wound up being oblivious to almost everything else, including the fact that rather than the hotel restaurant, they were being ushered to the hotel ballroom that was ordinarily closed to the general public.

His mother was still plying Elizabeth with the typical first-encounter questions—"So where did you and my son meet?"—when the doors to the ballroom parted and one hundred and fifty of his parents' closest friends and relatives all shouted out in unison: "Surprise!"

Somehow, she remained oblivious.

It took his father, physically grasping his mother's head and gently turning it so that she was actually looking into the ballroom rather than at Elizabeth, before what was transpiring actually registered for the woman.

With a stunned gasp, followed by a squeal of delight, Adriana finally comprehended exactly what was happening. But even then, she assumed that Elizabeth was who her son had said she was—until Elizabeth disengaged herself from the hold the older woman had on her arm, politely telling her that "I really have to go join the ensemble now, Mrs. Winterset."

"What does she mean, Jared?" his mother had asked, looking rather confused.

That was when he'd told his mother that Elizabeth was a violinist he'd hired to play at their party. The very first violinist, he emphasized, adding that the people within the ensemble had been handpicked by her. Elizabeth, he told her, had an excellent ear for blending.

Though her expression didn't change, he could see by the look in his mother's electric-blue eyes that her utter delight over the surprise party had waned just the slightest touch.

Soon, Mom, soon, he'd silently promised the woman. He intended to have Elizabeth become exactly what he'd told his mother she was when he'd made the initial introduction.

But first he needed to tell Elizabeth, he thought with a rueful smile. After all, it was only fair that she be forearmed with this information—that he had fallen in love with her—before he informed his mother how he felt and have her make a beeline for Elizabeth as he knew she would.

In all his wild imaginings, he'd never thought that he'd find someone who he wanted to spend the rest of his life with. Moreover, he'd always felt that what his parents had was not just special, but exceedingly rare as well. To believe that lightning could strike not once but twice within the same family, well, that was the stuff that Hollywood movies were made out of. It didn't happen in real life.

And yet, she made him want to take a chance, to set his sights on something loftier than just the end of the week with the same woman he'd begun it with.

"It's a wonderful party," his mother told him with enthusiasm when he stopped by their table to see if there was anything that either one of his parents might need.

"Yes," his father zealously agreed, clearly touched that so many people had turned out to help them celebrate this milestone. "Thank you, son."

"Megan set everything in motion before she left," Jared reminded his parents.

"She's a good girl, too," his mother commented, then seemed compelled to say, "But you know what would make this wonderful party even better—?"

"Adriana." His father's voice rose ever so slightly in a partial warning note. Having shared so much of their lives together, Matthew Winterset apparently knew *exactly* what his wife was thinking and where she was going with the thought she was voicing.

She looked at her husband, the soul of innocence. "I'm just saying, Matthew…" She deliberately allowed her voice to trail off without finishing her sentence.

"I think we *all* know what you're saying, honey," his father said, fondly brushing a kiss to her forehead.

Granted Adriana had a few annoying habits, but so did Matthew. It was, and always had been, the bottom line that counted. And the bottom line in this case was that everyone knew Matthew loved this woman. But he seemed to love her more when she refrained from voicing certain recurring sentiments.

Lacing his fingers through hers, Matthew coaxed, "C'mon, let's dance, honey."

"Yes, dear," she murmured, gracefully rising to her feet.

Jared watched his parents walk onto the dance floor, then meld into one being as they defined one another with their fluid movements.

Dancing. That was, Jared thought, a very tempting idea.

So far, he hadn't had a single dance with Elizabeth, although he'd been on the dance floor a number of times. But each and every time it had been with one of his relatives. There had been his father's widowed sister, Aunt Alicia, and then he'd taken a turn with several of his younger cousins because they had all come without a "plus one" in tow.

He'd even attempted one dance with Megan, but halfway through she had cut it short, flagging and saying if she didn't sit down, her ankles and feet would swell up like balloons.

That was *more* than enough to persuade him to escort his sister back to her table—and her husband who had wisely chosen not to dance tonight—posthaste.

And, as irony would have it, the one woman who had captured his fancy had not been available so far. He intended to do something to remedy that.

Jared crossed the dance floor, making his way over to the ensemble. Coming to a stop beside Elizabeth, his intended target, he said, "Any chance of you taking a break while the rest of your friends go on playing?"

This was almost like the first time she'd laid eyes on him, Elizabeth thought. Chills kept insisting on running up and down her spine. Was it because of her attraction, or was it because she had already initiated the program that would ultimately result in her being alone again?

She just didn't know.

"Sorry," she told Jared, "I'm afraid it's one for all and all for one. Either we all take a break, or we all play," she informed him, having every intention of spending the entire evening seated right where she was even *during* a band break.

"That's okay, Liz, we can play one number without you, right, guys?" Amanda spoke up, looking at the other musicians. "After all, you were the one who got us this gig," she tossed in just in case someone did feel like protesting.

"Yeah, go ahead. Take a break," Jack echoed, although with a note of reluctance. "We'll muddle through without you just this once," he grumbled.

Elizabeth hoped that the keyboardist's parting shot didn't mean he still carried a torch for her, but she shoved that unsettling notion aside when the other two musicians graciously urged her to go enjoy herself.

Jared reclaimed her hand. "I do believe majority rules," he announced as he took her hand in his, coaxing her to her feet.

Not wanting to cause a scene, Elizabeth allowed herself to be led off as the rest of the ensemble struck up the chords for the old Etta James standard "At Last."

Elizabeth got the point immediately—and prayed that Jared wouldn't.

Struggling against feeling like someone being auctioned off to the highest bidder, Elizabeth shot Amanda an if-looks-could-kill kind of look.

The latter was the personification of smiling innocence as she continued playing.

"I think it's going really well, don't you?" Jared asked her as he swayed in time to the rhythm.

Why did she get the feeling he was saying more than it seemed?

Because she felt herself walking on extremely shaky ground, she tried to nail down his meaning and hoped for the best.

"Yes, the party seems like a huge success. Congratulations, Jared." She whispered the words a tad too close to his ear, her voice raspy and, consequently, sounding sexier than hell. It made him want to grab her hand, and run off with the rest of her.

"And so's the ensemble," he emphasized for good measure—and because they were actually better than he had even hoped.

"They're a very good bunch of musicians," Elizabeth agreed, for the moment comfortable because she was on familiar, not to mention neutral, ground.

"I heard my uncle say something about possibly hiring them to play for this party he's going to be having for himself—he's retiring in a couple of months," Jared added, giving her as much information as he had right now. He just wanted to be sure that he had her services reserved for that particular evening.

He was about to give her the exact date when she

interrupted him. "I'll get you all of their cards," she promised.

"Why would I need the cards if I have you?" he wanted to know, a little perplexed.

When she looked up at him sharply, he had the uneasy feeling that he was being given notice—without so much as a word actually being exchanged between them to that effect.

He felt even more certain of that when she insisted, "Take the cards, anyway."

"All right," he agreed, plucking them out of her hand, "if it'll make you happy."

It was her turn to look at him quizzically. Just what did he mean by that? "My happiness has nothing to do with it."

"Now, there we might have a slight point of disagreement," he told her.

But just then, the song ended and Elizabeth took her cue, quickly evacuating the dance floor.

It seemed to Jared that she was actually relieved to have the dance over with. He was even more certain when she cheerfully announced, "Well, my reprieve's over. Time for me to get back."

Jared was about to say something to stop her, but someone behind him called out his name. By the time he finally turned back, he'd found that she had all but vanished on him.

Elizabeth had taken the opportunity his momentary distraction had provided and quickly hurried back to the ensemble.

For now, her safe haven.

Something was definitely off, Jared thought, going

to rejoin some friends. He was, quite frankly, mystified as to what was going on with Elizabeth—or why she was behaving so strangely.

The feeling that something wasn't right grew stronger. Try as he might, he wasn't able to get Elizabeth alone at the party; she was always too busy. He supposed he could understand that; she had a great deal she felt responsible for.

And when the celebration was finally over and the guests began to leave, to Jared's surprise Elizabeth seemed to just disappear before his very eyes. He'd been positive that she would remain until the very end, staying with him until he was ready to leave.

But she hadn't.

Then it got worse.

When he called Elizabeth on her cell, and then her landline, both just went straight to voice mail.

He was starting to get worried.

After several days, he still wasn't able to get hold of her.

And when he came by her apartment, he found that it was shrouded in darkness. No one was home. He waited for hours, but she never came home.

Had she gone out of town on a gig? Or left on vacation? While both were perfectly plausible possibilities, he didn't like to think that either had taken place, at least not without Elizabeth telling him. They had shared almost three very arousing, incredible weeks together and now, nothing.

Had he just imagined that they had something going between them, or had something else happened?

At his wit's end, not knowing where else to turn, he went to see Theresa Manetti, approaching her in the small shop where she took her catering orders.

Surprised to see him so soon, before she could ask, "How's everything?" he told her.

It was definitely *not* what she expected to hear.

"Elizabeth's disappeared?" Theresa asked incredulously.

In all the matches she and her friends had brought together, both jointly and singularly, this had never happened before.

Too restless to sit down at the small table where contracts were drawn up and heavenly confections were sampled, Jared paced about the small shop.

"It certainly seems that way to me," he told her helplessly. "I've driven by Elizabeth's apartment several times. She doesn't answer the door, and there're never any lights on. I've tried her cell and her landline, but they all go to voice mail. I've left over a dozen messages and she hasn't returned a single one. The last time I called, some recording told me her inbox was full."

He looked at Theresa, silently clamoring for her help. "Elizabeth didn't say anything about leaving town, and, frankly, I'm beginning to worry that something happened to her."

Jared was just a couple of years younger than her own son and her heart went out to him.

"I would, too," she agreed sympathetically. Here, at least, she could set his mind at ease, at least partially. "But as it happens, I know her father and I had occasion to see him yesterday. He didn't mention anything about Elizabeth, good or bad, and I know he would have if there was something to report either way."

She saw the skepticism in Jared's eyes and knew exactly what he was thinking. That sometimes parents were the last to know.

But not in this case.

"As I'm sure you know…Elizabeth's father lost his wife when Elizabeth was very young. He was determined that she and her brothers wouldn't grow up feeling as if they'd somehow been abandoned. He's very close to his children," she informed Jared.

Reminded of their strong family bond, Jared decided to get in contact with Elizabeth's father. If, for some reason, she had decided not to see him anymore, then, painful though it was, he needed to know that, too.

"Would you mind giving me his phone number?" he asked Theresa.

It was, Theresa felt, the very least she could do.

"Of course, Jared. Just let me get my address book." She paused when she saw the slightly inquisitive look on the young man's troubled face. Theresa flashed him a smile. "I know, an address book sounds hopelessly old-fashioned, but I feel better about writing things down. Power failures and dead batteries don't affect things written down in books and that way, other than occasionally misplacing it, I don't have to worry about losing the phone numbers and addresses of my best customers. Like you," she added on with a wink before she slipped into her tiny back office to retrieve the aforementioned address book.

Behind her, she heard Jared sigh. It was one of the saddest sounds she'd ever heard.

Chapter Sixteen

When he saw Elizabeth crossing the floor of the busy restaurant, walking just slightly behind the hostess, John Stephens found himself wondering if he was witnessing an end of a beloved tradition. If, once the dust eventually settled, she would still be able to make a little time for him.

Or if marriage would change her.

Well, that—including the matter of marriage—remained to be seen, but the survival of their Thursday night tradition wasn't the important thing here, he reminded himself. There was something a great deal more pressing to deal with.

As was his habit, John rose ever so slightly in his seat, a sign of politeness and his strict upbringing even though the young woman slipping into her seat was his daughter.

"I wasn't certain you'd come," he mused with a smile as he settled back in his seat.

"Why?" She accepted the menu from the hostess with a nod. "It's Thursday and we do have a standing date for dinner on Thursdays," she said. "And, except for that one time—"

She let her voice trail off, not wanting to think about that recent interlude. It was in the past now, where it belonged. And she was moving on.

She really was.

Anytime now...

"Why are you staying at Amanda's apartment instead of your place?" he asked, clearly surprising Elizabeth. "That area isn't all that safe at night. By the way, I hear the chef has prepared the veal scaloppine in a new way. You might like it."

The casual remark did not erase the impact of her father's question. She stared at him. "How did you know I was staying at Amanda's? And how do you even *know* where Amanda lives?"

To her best recollection, she'd never given him Amanda's address. There had been no reason to.

"I called around," he told her vaguely. "You forget, your brother Ethan had a crush on Amanda not that long ago. He gave me her address." He paused to skim the menu before making up his mind. "She's lost a lot of weight since college," he commented casually, the doctor in him coming out. "But fortunately, it suits her."

It was just one surprise after another tonight, wasn't it? "You're checking up on me?" Elizabeth asked, astonished. This was *not* the sort of relationship she was accustomed to having with her father.

"Just making sure you were all right, that's all," he corrected. As he placed the menu on the table for a moment, his eyes met hers. "Just because an offspring reaches the age to legally vote…doesn't mean a father automatically stops worrying. Parents continue to worry about their progeny until they draw their last breath."

"Does that 'last breath' passage belong to the parent or the child?" she asked suspiciously.

"Either." John took a sip of the one glass of red wine he allowed himself with his dinner. And then, just like that, he changed the subject. "You'll never guess who called on me the other day."

Since her father knew enough people to populate a small state, guessing who that "someone" had been could become a full-time project for the next year and a half. Rather than even try, she gamely asked, "Who?"

"That young man who threw his parents an anniversary party."

Never in a million years would she have even thought to say Jared's name. She stared at her father, nearly speechless.

Finally, she was able to utter, "You're kidding."

"I do kid on occasion," Dr. Stephens admitted freely, "but this is not one of those occasions. He was worried about you, the young man," he clarified. "Very worried. When he couldn't find you, he went looking for me to find out if you were all right. A man like that," he told his daughter, pinning her in place with a look, "is well worth knowing." Finished with the menu, he set it off to the side. "We talked for a while. He seems like a very nice young man, Elizabeth. Decent and thoughtful," he added, watching his daughter's face for some sort of sign as to how she felt, although he was fairly certain he knew.

Avoiding his eyes, she stared at her napkin instead. "He is," she told her father quietly.

"I see. And yet you have decided to pull a disappearing act on this young man because…?" he asked, waiting to hear what sort of an excuse she had come up with.

How could he even ask, after what she'd watched him go through all those years ago? And even now, he still elected to remain alone and not even so much as attempt dating another woman.

"Because I don't want to get hurt, Dad, okay?" she fired back a bit testily.

He had done his homework, speaking to Theresa Manetti about the young man in question. Everything he had learned recently told him that the woman had made a very good choice when she'd recommended Jared Winterset as someone who would be good for his daughter and would always treat her well.

But for the sake of moving the situation along, he pretended to know nothing. "Then he didn't treat you well," he surmised.

She wasn't about to lie. "No, he treated me very well."

Her father went on to the next logical assumption. "But you just don't like him."

She lowered her eyes again, pretending to read the menu. "No, I do," she admitted very softly, feeling fresh wounds beginning to open up again.

John put it all together for his daughter. "Then if he treats you well and you like him—and he obviously likes you after all the trouble he's gone to in order to find me—I fail to see why you have suddenly decided to understudy Houdini."

She closed her eyes for a moment, feeling tears of frustration gathering just beneath her lids. "Because I remember what you went through when Mom died, that's why," she answered hoarsely.

"You remember," he repeated thoughtfully. "Then you also remember how having you and your brothers around gave me a reason to live, a reason to go on. And you also remember all the happy, rich moments that existed in our home when your mother was still alive, still well." His voice welled with emotion. "I wouldn't have traded one moment of that brief time together for a lifetime of uninspired tranquillity free of any gut-wrenching pain."

The waiter approached their table, ready to take their orders, but John waved him back.

"Soon, but not yet," he told the young man. Leaning over the table as the waiter retreated, he took Elizabeth's hand in his own. "Oh, my darling daughter, you have no idea how incredibly fortunate I felt, finding your mother. And how very rare it is when two truly kindred souls actually manage to discover one another.

"If you and Jared *are* kindred souls, don't turn your back on what you can have out of fear that it won't last a lifetime. No matter how short a time it *does* last, I promise you, it will *fill* your lifetime." A fond smile curved his mouth as he remembered his life back then. "Loving your mother made me feel alive for the first time in my life, and the short time I had with her gave me three wonderful children who make my life worth living," he told her with her quiet emotion.

She swallowed hard, deeply moved by what her dad was saying, and nodded at him to continue.

"If I had only one wish for you, Elizabeth, it would be that you embrace what is there right in front of you and savor it for as long as you have it. Your heart will thank you for it. *Always.*"

And then he turned and signaled the waiter. The food server came alert and headed back to their table. "We're ready to place our orders now," he told the young man.

Okay, no question about it, Jared decided as he stopped what he was doing to listen again. He was definitely going crazy.

There really wasn't any other conclusion for him to reach. Ever since Elizabeth had walked out on him—and there was no other way to view her sudden disappearing act once he knew she was all right—he'd tried to literally bury himself in his work. His goal was to keep so busy that he didn't have time to dwell on the loneliness that was eating away at him.

Loneliness that had never existed before Elizabeth came into his life.

So maybe what he was hearing now, slaving away in his office after hours on another major national ad campaign, was just a product of his encroaching exhaustion.

Why else would he be hearing music when everything, except for the somewhat anemic heating unit, was shut down?

And not just music, *violin* music.

The kind that Elizabeth played.

You'd think at least his mind would be on his side instead of slowly driving him insane, unhinging him like this, he thought.

He sighed, abandoning his work and dragging both hands through his hair in abject frustration.

Maybe, he decided, he should just go home and get drunk, or try to erase Elizabeth from his mind for at least a few hours by popping a couple of sleeping pills to help him get some rest.

The only problem with that was that he didn't *have* a couple of sleeping pills. He'd never had trouble sleeping before she'd upended his life.

All right, then, maybe if—

Damn it, that *did* sound so real. And so close.

To prove to himself that he was imagining all this, that there *was* no music, Jared pushed himself back from his desk.

Walking out of his glass-enclosed inner office, he threw open the outer door leading into the corridor.

That was when he stopped dead.

He was not only *hearing* things, but now he was *seeing* them as well.

Right?

Even though he knew she had to be a product of his overworked brain, he heard himself ask uncertainly, "Elizabeth?"

She'd stopped playing the moment the door had opened. It was very hard to play, she discovered, with your heart backed up in your throat.

"Hi," she whispered in a barely audible voice. "Have any requests?"

"Yes," he said, still not a hundred percent sure he

wasn't carrying on a conversation with some complex hallucination. "I want answers, like, what are you doing here?"

"Playing the violin." The simple reply sounded almost flippant to her ear, so Elizabeth added, "Trying to make amends by serenading you."

"Serenading me," he echoed incredulously.

She nodded. "It's really the only way I know to show you how very deeply sorry I am. I let the violin speak for me." *And hope it's enough,* she added silently.

Jared's eyes never left hers. She could almost *feel* them delving into her soul. He was neither smiling nor frowning. His expression was entirely unreadable and that in turn made her feel very nervous.

It also made her think that she might have just willfully destroyed her chances of ever attaining paradise. Because, belatedly, she realized that was what life with him would have meant.

Paradise.

"I'd rather you spoke, not played," he said.

It took her a long moment to find her courage. "I was afraid," she finally told him after a beat. "I know it sounds stupid, but I was afraid," she repeated. "Afraid I loved you too much, afraid that losing you would destroy me the way I thought losing my mother had destroyed my father."

"I met your father," he replied in a voice still devoid of any emotion. "He didn't seem all that destroyed to me."

"That's because his love for my mother made him strong," she explained. She hadn't realized that before, but now, it seemed so obvious. How could she have missed that? "He told me that. He also said something to the effect that the precious moments he'd spent with my mother was worth far more than an entire lifetime of bland, cocooned safety. He advised me to seize what I was lucky enough to have—if I still have it," she added, deliberately looking at Jared and waiting for him to tell her, one way or another, if her apology had come too late to do any good.

If she had hurt him too much to be forgiven.

Rather than answer her directly, Jared took her by the hand and led her back into his office.

Closing the door, still maintaining a distance between them, he began to speak. He started by bringing up the past, just as she had done.

"My father once told me that when he first saw my mother, he just knew. Knew that she was different. Knew that she was special. That she was, in effect, 'the one.' The one he wanted to spend the rest of his life with.

"Until just recently, I thought it was just some nice little bedtime story he'd woven together for Megan and me when we were kids. A fairy-tale love story that had very little truth in it. But now I realize that it actually *can* happen. That sometimes, if you're very, very lucky, lightning *does* strike you and your path actually *does* cross with the one you were meant to be with. *Destined* to be with," he emphasized.

Elizabeth blew out a shaky breath. Part of her was more afraid than she'd ever been in her life. Afraid to hope that he was offering her everything she'd ever wanted. And still afraid in some deep part of herself that if he was saying what she hoped he was saying and she in turn said yes, that she *would* be leaving herself open to an entire world of hurt.

But practically, if she said no, if she suddenly still retreated and walked away in order to stay "protected," how much less would she ache? How much less would she really hurt?

She suspected that the damage was already done.

This way, at least she would get to build up a stock-pile of happy memories first, before she had her heart ripped out from her chest.

And who knew? Maybe she'd be even luckier and never feel the grief of death because she would be the first to go, not him.

It was risky, but there was at least a fighting chance of coming out ahead if she took a chance on love. At any rate, she'd be condemned to a life of eternal sorrow and regret if she continued to play it safe.

"So, what are you saying?" she asked. "That you want me back?"

"No, not 'back.' I never gave you up to begin with. I want you for forever, Elizabeth. I want you until the day one of us dies, and hopefully that won't be for a very long time." Well, he'd placed all his cards on the table. It was time to find out if he was destined to be a winner, or a loser. "What do you say?"

She felt as if she were dreaming.

But if she were dreaming, would she be trembling this way? Would her heart be overflowing with such incredible joy?

She ran her tongue along her lips before she answered, afraid they would stick together in midword. "You make it very hard to say no."

"Lady, I'm going to make it impossible to say no," he promised her firmly.

She couldn't help teasing him, now that she finally realized that all her wishes could come true. "You know, in some states that's called stalking."

Unfazed, he countered with, "And in other states, it's telling you that I'll love you until the day I die."

"You love me," she repeated incredulously. That was the only logical upshot of all this, but she was having trouble fathoming the reason. After all, he really hadn't said anything about having feelings for her before. On the contrary, he'd made it seem that if he couldn't have the perfect relationship, he didn't want any at all. "Why?"

"Because I'm into self-torture," he said drily. "Why do you think?" he asked. When she didn't answer, he told her. "Because even though you ran over my self-esteem with a steamroller, you are still the most exciting, the most intelligent, most wonderful woman I have ever known, and my life feels as if all the lights have gone out of the world whenever you're not around."

Oh God, how had she gotten to be so lucky? she wondered. "Yes!" she cried out loud.

"Yes?" Just what was she saying yes to? That she agreed with him, that she would stay with him, that she would marry him or that she knew she was the power source in his life?

"Yes," she breathed again. "To everything. Most of all," she said, weaving her arms around his neck, "yes to you."

He smiled into her eyes, relieved and happier than he'd ever been. "I can live with that."

"As long as you live with me, everything else is just icing," she murmured.

"I've always had a weakness for icing," he said just before he sealed his lips to hers.

* * * * *

REQUEST YOUR FREE BOOKS!

2 FREE NOVELS PLUS 2 FREE GIFTS!

⊕ HARLEQUIN®

SPECIAL EDITION

Life, Love & Family

YES! Please send me 2 FREE Harlequin® Special Edition novels and my 2 FREE gifts (gifts are worth about $10). After receiving them, if I don't wish to receive any more books, I can return the shipping statement marked "cancel." If I don't cancel, I will receive 6 brand-new novels every month and be billed just $4.49 per book in the U.S. or $5.24 per book in Canada. That's a savings of at least 14% off the cover price! It's quite a bargain! Shipping and handling is just 50¢ per book in the U.S. and 75¢ per book in Canada.* I understand that accepting the 2 free books and gifts places me under no obligation to buy anything. I can always return a shipment and cancel at any time. Even if I never buy another book, the two free books and gifts are mine to keep forever.

235/335 HDN FVTV

Name	(PLEASE PRINT)	
Address		Apt. #
City	State/Prov.	Zip/Postal Code

Signature (if under 18, a parent or guardian must sign)

Mail to the Harlequin® Reader Service:
IN U.S.A.: P.O. Box 1867, Buffalo, NY 14240-1867
IN CANADA: P.O. Box 609, Fort Erie, Ontario L2A 5X3

Want to try two free books from another line?
Call 1-800-873-8635 or visit www.ReaderService.com.

* Terms and prices subject to change without notice. Prices do not include applicable taxes. Sales tax applicable in N.Y. Canadian residents will be charged applicable taxes. Offer not valid in Quebec. This offer is limited to one order per household. Not valid for current subscribers to Harlequin Special Edition books. All orders subject to credit approval. Credit or debit balances in a customer's account(s) may be offset by any other outstanding balance owed by or to the customer. Please allow 4 to 6 weeks for delivery. Offer available while quantities last.

Your Privacy—The Harlequin® Reader Service is committed to protecting your privacy. Our Privacy Policy is available online at www.ReaderService.com or upon request from the Harlequin Reader Service.

We make a portion of our mailing list available to reputable third parties that offer products we believe may interest you. If you prefer that we not exchange your name with third parties, or if you wish to clarify or modify your communication preferences, please visit us at www.ReaderService.com/consumerschoice or write to us at Harlequin Reader Service Preference Service, P.O. Box 9062, Buffalo, NY 14269. Include your complete name and address.

HSE13

In Buckshot Hills, Texas, a sexy doctor meets his match in the least likely woman—a beautiful cowgirl looking to reinvent herself....

Enjoy a sneak peek from USA TODAY bestselling author Judy Duarte's new Harlequin® Special Edition® story, TAMMY AND THE DOCTOR *,the first book in* Byrds of a Feather, *a brand-new miniseries launching in March 2013!*

***

Before she could comment or press Tex for more details, a couple of light knocks sounded at the door.

Her grandfather shifted in his bed, then grimaced. "Who is it?"

"Mike Sanchez."

Doc? Tammy's heart dropped to the pit of her stomach with a thud, then thumped and pumped its way back up where it belonged.

"Come on in," Tex said.

Thank goodness her grandfather had issued the invitation, because she couldn't have squawked out a single word.

As Doc entered the room, looking even more handsome than he had yesterday, Tammy struggled to remain cool and calm.

And it wasn't just her heartbeat going wacky. Her feminine hormones had begun to pump in a way they'd never pumped before.

"Good morning," Doc said, his gaze landing first on Tex, then on Tammy.

As he approached the bed, he continued to look at Tammy,

his head cocked slightly.

"What's the matter?" she asked.

"I'm sorry. It's just that your eyes are an interesting shade of blue. I'm sure you hear that all the time."

"Not really." And not from anyone who'd ever mattered. In truth, they were a fairly common color—like the sky or bluebonnets or whatever. "I've always thought of them as run-of-the-mill blue."

"There's nothing ordinary about it. In fact, it's a pretty shade."

The compliment set her heart on end. But before she could think of just the perfect response, he said, "If you don't mind stepping out of the room, I'd like to examine your grandfather."

Of course she minded leaving. She wanted to stay in the same room with Doc for the rest of her natural-born days. But she understood her grandfather's need for privacy.

"Of course." Apparently it was going to take more than simply batting her eyes to woo him, but there was no way Tammy would be able to pull off a makeover by herself. Maybe she could ask her beautiful cousins for help?

She had no idea what to say the next time she ran into them. But somehow, by hook or by crook, she'd have to think of something.

Because she was going to risk untold humiliation and embarrassment by begging them to turn a cowgirl into a lady!

***

Look for TAMMY AND THE DOCTOR from Harlequin® Special Edition® available March 2013

HARLEQUIN®

SPECIAL EDITION

Life, Love and Family

Coming in March 2013 from fan-favorite author

KATHLEEN EAGLE

Cowboy Jack McKenzie has a checkered past, but when rancher's daughter Lily reluctantly visits her father, he wants more than anything to show that he's a reformed man. Has she made up her mind too early that this would be a short stay at the ranch?

Look for *One Less Lonely Cowboy* next month from Kathleen Eagle.

Available March 2013 from Harlequin Special Edition wherever books are sold.

⬡ HARLEQUIN®

SPECIAL EDITION

Life, Love and Family

Look for the next book in
The Fortunes of Texas: Southern Invasion miniseries!

After a broken marriage, Asher Fortune moves to
Red Rock, where he needs someone to help him
and his four-year-old son, Jace, start a new life.
He knew upon their first meeting that Marnie was
great for Jace, but he didn't realize what was in
store for *him!*

A Small Fortune
by *USA TODAY* bestselling author
Marie Ferrarella

*Available March 2013 from Harlequin Special Edition
wherever books are sold.*

HSE657285

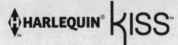

HARLEQUIN®

A *Romance* FOR EVERY MOOD™

**Stay up-to-date on all your
romance-reading news with the
Harlequin Shopping Guide,
featuring bestselling authors, exciting new
miniseries, books to watch and more!**

The newest issue will be delivered right to you
with our compliments! There are 4 each year.

Signing up is easy.

EMAIL

ShoppingGuide@Harlequin.ca

WRITE TO US

HARLEQUIN BOOKS
Attention: Customer Service Department
P.O. Box 9057, Buffalo, NY 14269-9057

OR PHONE

1-800-873-8635 in the United States
1-888-343-9777 in Canada

Please allow 4-6 weeks for delivery of the first issue by mail.